# THORNFIELD

# THORNFIELD

MEAGAN CLEVELAND

# PROLOGUE

## EX LIBRIS

If you stand at the top of the staircase in the Lowood Library, the building would appear empty, but if you head towards junior fiction and look down to the floor below you would see a slight figure encamped at the table by History A to C.

You might think the figure was sleeping from the listless roll of her head, the way her body sagged against the shelves, shoulders hunched inwards, the only movement the soft rise and fall of her chest. Upon closer inspection you would find a pair of large brown eyes fixed upon the book cradled in her arms, their irises dancing across the page while the girl drinks the information in. A pale hand would flutter out from beneath dark sleeves and the thin paper would sigh as its pages turn one after the other. You might wonder why the librarians have not yet chased the girl from the building now that it was near closing time. But as she reaches out a trembling hand you would notice that her skin is a canvas painted with blossoms of nasty purple thumbprints, the bruises painting the picture of the trouble at home. When the lights overhead begin to dim and flicker she resignedly closes the book and places it back upon the shelf. She gathers her things together and drifts out of the doors of her sanctuary like a shade.

It is a warm August night, summer is reluctant to relinquish its hold and give way to fall. The air is humid and heavy with expectation. The girl lifts her head as the wind tousles her hair. She looks out at the darkening sky, violet clouds gather overhead and she must hurry to get home before true darkness falls.

She hastens down the empty streets, the clip of her heels upon the pavement echoing around her. The trees stretch out their limbs, their leaves gilded with the first gold of autumn. Overhead a single leaf quivers and falls, soaring on the evening breeze and catching upon the screen door of a little house sitting on the lonely corner of a darkened road.

There is no light shining on the porch that night. Its absence indicating the displeasure of the woman waiting within. She lays awake in her bed, arms crossed, a frown tugging at the corner of her lips. When she hears the soft click of the lock she turns on her side, her eyes flutter closed and she feigns sleep. She hears her daughter's soft tread across the entryway, the creak of the stairs as she tiptoes up into her room. *Let her creep around*, the mother thinks. *I'll deal with her in the morning.*

The daughter holds her breath as she passes the bedroom across from hers, her eyes skipping to the gap under the door. Relief washes over her when she sees there is no light flooding from underneath. Its occupant is asleep.

She slowly nudges the door to her own room open and gently sets her books on her desk, her bag on the floor next to her chair. She undresses in the dark, not wanting to wake the rest of the house. She draws back the worn duvet and crawls underneath. She glances over at her night stand, marking the time.

She did not mean to stay so late at the library. She glances over at the stack of cardboard boxes towering in the corner of her room, waiting to be loaded into the rental car. She resolves to do it in the morning. She reaches for her clock to set an alarm for the morning when light suddenly pools beneath her door, limning her room in gold.

*He's awake.*

Shadows appear under the gap of the door, a pair of feet pacing back and forth. She holds her breath and watches them move, wishing fervently that they will go away, that they will disappear and let her sleep. When the shadows are gone she cannot suppress the sigh that escapes her, the relief a weight lifted from her chest. The confrontation she has been dreading has not come to pass. She turns on her side, facing the opposite direction from the door. She pulls the blanket over her shoulders and surrenders herself to sleep.

She is awoken by a thud.

She opens her eyes, puzzled by the light still leeching underneath the door, the stark shadows cast on the wall, silent witnesses to her confusion.

Slowly she props herself up and waits with baited breath, listening for some movement across the hall. Silence fills the room. She strains forward and can hear a faint moan. She clambers out of bed and pads across the room to her closed door, staring at her hand poised above the handle.

She knew something was bound to happen tonight. She knew he didn't want her to go, she knew he would struggle without her, that he would cause some argument, cause some scene to prevent her from leaving for good. She glances at the boxes stacked in the corner, thinks of what they represent.

A fresh start. A new life. She *has* to go. She turns from the door to head back to bed when she hears her mother stir. She listens to the familiar tread shuffle down the hallway, the floorboards creaking under her footsteps. Silently she gives thanks that her mother will deal with it, that she might rest and prepare for the journey tomorrow. She has just climbed back into bed, drawing her arms up around her head, her eyes fluttering closed, when she hears the scream.

Her blood runs cold. She bolts upright, tripping over the blankets that have wrapped around her legs like grasping hands. She lurches towards the door to throw it open, hurling herself across the hall.

Her mother's frame fills the doorway, the echo of her scream still resounding in the girl's head.

She reaches out a hand to place on her mother's shoulder but she has already moved, she has already thrown herself forward and suddenly the girl sees it all.

She sees the familiar disarray of her brother's room. Clean and dirty clothes alike are cast about the floor, movie posters are taped to the walls, superheroes glare down at her as she steps across the threshold. Light glints upon the blade of an x-acto knife laying upon the carpet, a pool of crimson gathering around it. Her brother's limp hand stretches out to her accusingly.

# CHAPTER ONE

## MOMENTO MORI

A girl is coming down a flight of stairs.

The stairway is narrow and smells of wet dog. The florescent lights flicker overhead, the walls covered by fluttering moths eager to get closer to that trembling light.

The girl moves hesitantly, the steps unfamiliar to her, hand trailing down the banister with whitened knuckles. She reaches the bottom and glances over her shoulder, trying to remember whether she locked the door. Anxiety rises in her throat like bile. She swallows it down and steps out.

The air is close and heavy, the grey clouds gathering overhead promise a storm. She is glad she grabbed her umbrella on her way out. She hitches her satchel higher on her shoulder and begins to walk from her apartment towards the campus.

The street is empty. Early morning light struggles to peek through the clouds. It is the type of day where one should stay in bed, a cup of hot tea in one hand, a well worn book in the other. But classes are starting soon and the girl is eager to make a good impression.

As she makes her way down the road the world starts to wake around her. Men in suits and ties shuffle out of the door, briefcases tucked under their arm. Young women in brightly coloured running shoes burst out the door. Tired couples amble past, juggling fussy babies as they fish for their keys to lock up behind them.

The girl has just mounted the steps to her building when the first drop of rain trickles from the clouds. Soon others follow suit and the soft patter of rain eases her nerves as she slips into Thornfield Hall.

The email sent by the department chair the week before said the Art History department is on the ground floor of the building. She pushes her way through a second set of heavy wooden doors and makes her way down a small flight of stairs. A long hallway dotted with wooden doors lays before her. She pads down the empty corridor, her flats scuffing on the old linoleum, and as she passes she reads the names on the doors along the way. She walks down the still hallway until she comes to a small door at the end. She reaches into her bag and withdraws a set of old brass keys and turns the lock. The lights flicker on and a room of four empty desks awaits her, the name *Charlotte Grey* taped onto the desk in the left hand corner.

Smiling she slings the bag from her shoulder and settles it on her chair. She reaches in and pulls out books, notebooks, pens and places them in a small pile in the centre of the desk. She decides to bring some postcards and drawings to personalize her desk the next time she comes in. She sits in the chair, legs dangling and spins around.

The four first year graduate students would be sharing this office and she is both anxious and eager to meet her cohort.

She glances at her watch. The orientation lunch is still hours away but anxiety makes early risers.

She reaches for one of her books and begins to read, hoping to ease the time until the luncheon. She loses herself in her book, too immersed in the life of an 18th century painter to notice the figure that enters the doorway behind her. A *thud* makes her jump and turn around. Another girl has claimed the desk opposite hers, the name *Adele Sheridan* taped to its wooden shelves. Charlotte looks at the other girl, feeling slightly dismayed. Now that is what a graduate student should look like, polished and professional. The girl's blonde hair falls perfectly straight, the blunt ends skimming her shoulders, the bow of her green silk blouse brightening her face. She smiles at Charlotte.

"Hi," She says brightly, grinning as she leans against the wall across from Charlotte. "I'm Adele."

"Charlotte." She waves and smiles timidly back.

"You nervous about the lunch too? Why else would we arrive half an hour early." She laughs and drops into her chair. She braces a hand against her desk and pushes so her chair glides across the room to settle in front of Charlotte, startling a laugh out of the other girl.

"Yes, I am a little nervous," she replies in her quiet voice. "I got here an hour ago."

Adele nods in understanding. She leans closer and squints at the books on Charlotte's desk.

"Goya!" She exclaims. "Love his stuff. Pretty dark though."

"It is a little." Charlotte agrees. "But that is why it is so interesting! He does commissioned work as well as explore the horrors of war and the human psyche."

Adele nods. "I get it. I'm into the Dutch masters myself," she says as she rummages through her back pack and withdraws a binder full of prints. She pulls one out of its sleeve to hold it aloft: a print of a still life of flowers and a skull atop a table. The centre of the bouquet is bright and vibrant, however, the flowers on the outer edges are withered and grey, the head of one of the roses on the table, captured in paint the moment it fell, still in full bloom, but soon to decay. A skull lies atop a leather bound book, the sockets of its empty eyes look away from the reminder of life and death beside it. Beneath the print are the words Adriaen van Utrecht *Vanitas Still Life with Bouquet and Skull*.

"*Momento mori.*" Charlotte murmurs.

Adele replies in a deep voice, "Remember you will die." Her serious demeanour changes like quicksilver, a smile brightens her face and she laughs. "I love that stuff." She smiles fondly at the print and sticks it to the cork board at the back of her desk. She looks over her shoulder at Charlotte and winks. "A reminder for both of us." Charlotte laughs as Adele waves her over. "Want to help?" She brandishes her binder of prints in one hand, a jar of pins in the other. Charlotte rises eagerly from her chair and together the two girls make a collage on the cork board. *Vanitas* takes pride of place as the largest of the prints, and Charlotte arranges a number of smaller prints beside it: Albrecht Dürer's *Four Horsemen of the Apocalypse*, Carel Fabritius's *The Goldfinch*, Rembrandt's *The Anatomy Lesson of Dr. Nicolaes Tulp*, and Johannes Vermeer's *Girl with a Pearl Earring*. Adele also pins up poems by Rilke and Goethe and photos of her with a group of friends. Charlotte glances wistfully at these photos, wishing that she had more photos of her friends before they drifted out of her life. She would only have art to pin on her desk.

As the girls pin the last photo in place a timer goes off.

"Time to go!" Adele laughs. She straightens her blouse and pats her hair. "Am I presentable?" Charlotte nods. "Good. Come on." Adele turns on her heel and marches out the door. Charlotte drifts after her, remembering to turn and lock the door behind her. She looks over her shoulder to see that Adele hasn't waited for her, she is halfway down the hall already. Charlotte sprints to catch up.

"Do you know where we have to go?" She pants, silently cursing that she did not look at her phone to confirm the room number for the luncheon.

"Yeah, its over here in the conference room." She nods ahead to an expanse of glass walls. Behind the glass is a gathering of faculty and grad students. Charlotte feels panic rise in her throat and swallows hard. She wonders if Adele hears. The other girl gives her a bright smile and places a hand on her arm. "Come on, I'll introduce you."

"How do you know them already?"

"Oh, didn't I mention it? I did my undergrad here too. Hey, Joanna!" She says this quickly, already turning to address the figure standing by the door, nursing a paper cup of coffee in her hands. The girl is tall with a cloud of tightly coiled dark hair, frowning as she looks around the room. Her frown deepens as she glances at Charlotte, no doubt taking in her frizzy hair, the ill fitting trousers she bought from the thrift store, the knees of the plaid pants already worn thin. She has to look the part of a successful grad student. Maybe then the others wouldn't see how unprepared for her new life she really feels.

As she feels the weight of the other girl's scrutiny Charlotte crosses her arms self consciously. She stands by silently as Adele chats with the other girl, shifting her weight from one foot to the other. The points of her oxfords pinch painfully at her toes while the backs cut into the delicate skin of her ankles. She tries not to grimace. She should have listened to her mother and wore the shoes around the apartment to break them in before her first day. A flash of a pale hand floats in her mind and she closes her eyes against it. She should have listened to her mother about a lot of things, really.

"Charlotte?"

She opens her eyes to see Adele and the other girl staring at her. Charlotte plasters a smile on her face, "Sorry, I have a bit of a headache. What did you say?

"I was just introducing you to Joanna! Joanna is a second year grad student, in fact she was one of the TAs of my last class as an undergrad."

Joanna rolls her eyes. "And what a class it was."

Adele laughs. "Yeah, it was crazy. So intense! It was a course on the High Renaissance with Professor O'Farrell. His class was amazing."

"Amazingly difficult," Joanna cuts in sharply. "He may be brilliant but he's a real asshole. You are lucky you didn't get him for your TA assignment." She tells Adele, turning away from Charlotte entirely.

"What was so difficult about it?" Charlotte asks. Joanna glances at her with a smirk.

"You'll see."

Dread turns her blood cold.

"What do you mean?"

Still smirking, Joanna nods to the table in the centre of the room.

"Go see."

Charlotte drifts away from the other girls and heads to the table. A row of books is laid out on its surface. Atop each book is a slip of paper bearing two names. The names of the grad students and the professors they would be working as teaching assistants to.

Charlotte finds her name soon enough atop a book about the High Renaissance. The name below hers reads Dr. Ellis O'Farrell.

# CHAPTER TWO

## ALMA MATER

Charlotte stares at the name on that small slip of paper, feeling anxiety rise in her throat. She closes her eyes a moment, inhaling, holding the breath, and then exhaling. She opens her eyes and reaches for the books.

Hurrying past Joanna and Adele she says "I'm just going to put these in the office. I'll be right back."

She can scarcely breathe as she flies down the hall until, finally, she is in the safety of the office. She shuts the door and sags against it.

It will be fine. Everything will be fine. Dr. O' Farrell can't be as bad as Joanna made him out to be.

She stares at the slip of paper in her hands until the words flow together, her own name combined with Dr. O' Farrell's. She drops the book atop her desk and presses the heels of her hands into her eyes.

She can't fall apart over something so trivial. She sacrificed so much to be here, she *has* to succeed. She plasters a smile on her face and opens the door.

She takes her time walking back to the conference room, soaking in the atmosphere of the old building.

Thornfield Hall was founded 1847, its gothic architecture

ivy covered and imposing. The old exterior gives the campus a sense of authority, while its interior is renovated to match the needs of this century. Its halls as white and sterile as a hospital ward. On the walls are posters of upcoming events at the campus or abroad, mixed in with news articles of the latest research of the faculty, award winning students grinning fixedly at the camera. Thornfield is a school for the successful and they want you to know it.

Her undergrad is just as old as Thornfield but does not have the same prestige, or the same funding. Its insides matched the outsides, the wood doors warped so badly they wouldn't close, the fluorescent lights overhead spurt on and off, the constant buzz of electricity a familiar headache. Freezing in the winter and boiling in the summer. Thornfield is cutting edge in comparison, a step up in the world, where the Art History department has an entire floor with its own library, a stark contrast to the three small offices the Art History professors occupied in a narrow corridor of cells, rather than the spacious offices at Thornfield. Her choice of graduate school is definitely an upgrade.

She is determined to give herself an upgrade as well. She drifted through much of her undergrad as a faceless student number, a vehicle to pay tuition, an automaton to submit essays and exams rather than a human being. She felt invisible. She desperately wants to feel more substantial during grad school, to become a student Thornfield would remember, a student they would celebrate even. She promises herself that this time she would do it right, this time she would focus on more than just her coursework. She wouldn't be so shy, she'd make friends, she'd join clubs, she would leave her mark. And she couldn't do that by hiding out in the grad office.

The conference room is buzzing with conversation when she returns. Adele spots her and waves her over, setting her drink down and leaning over to speak to her.

"Are you okay? You looked like you were having a panic attack."

Charlotte laughs shakily in reply. "I'm fine."

"You sure?" She places a hand on Charlotte's forearm. "Don't listen to Joanna, she is just trying to scare you. Dr. Ellis isn't that bad. He's tough, but fair. Just wait until you hear him lecture, he's really amazing. Working with him will be a great experience. You'll see."

Charlotte feels someone brush against her arm and she turns to find a very glamorous woman standing at her side. Her hair is a brilliant shade of orange, teased into a beehive, her large eyes framed by black cat's eyes glasses with rhinestones in the corners. She smiles broadly at the two girls.

"Hello. Adele I already know," she nods towards Adele and then turns back to Charlotte. "But I believe we haven't met. I'm Dr. Catherine Fairfax, but please, call me Cat," She extends a hand with long, red lacquered nails.

"Nice to meet you Dr. Fairfax, I mean Cat," Charlotte sputters as she shakes her hand. "I'm Charlotte."

"Just the girl I was looking for!" She laughs at the look of alarm that flashes across Charlotte's face. "No need to worry! I just wanted to let you know how much I enjoyed your entrance essay on Goya. As your focus of study deals with similar themes to my own, I've volunteered to be your advisor."

     MEAGAN CLEVELAND

"That's great!" Charlotte replies and stands in awe as Cat tells her about the book she has been working on about Artemisia Gentileschi. Charlotte feels herself relax as she listens. This is where she is meant to be, she can do this and she will succeed.

"Well, it was lovely meeting you but I had better go."

"Before you go, would you point out Dr. O' Farrell to me?"

"Oh, Ellis isn't in today, he's speaking at a conference and isn't due back until next week. Don't worry, you'll run into each other long before your first class."

Charlotte nods, but feels unease churn in her stomach.

She leaves her corner and drifts around the conference room introducing herself to the faculty and the other grad students. Finally, everyone begins to drift out of the conference room, the long table now devoid of snacks and complimentary coffee and tea. Charlotte finds Adele waiting for her by the door.

"How'd it go? Feeling better about everything?"

"Much better."

The two girls chat in the office for a while. Once Adele leaves, Charlotte reaches for her bag and her phone tumbles out. The screen flashes. Six missed calls. Charlottes swipes and watches the notifications disappear. She shoves the phone back into her bag and the office light goes out as she closes the door. Her umbrella lays forgotten beneath her desk.

Still jittering with the excitement of the day, Charlotte does not turn down the road to her apartment, instead she keeps walking. She walks to the borders of the university town and out into the country where a winding road cuts through fields of tangled grass.

Today is hard for her. She feels as if she is doing a performance of the person they think she should be, not who she really is, and it is exhausting.

The further she moves away from town the thicker the air becomes, fog gathering around her until she disappears into the mist.

# CHAPTER THREE

## DEUS EX MACHINA

The wind shrieks across the empty plain, a warning cry of what is yet to come. A winding black road cuts through the landscape like a scar. The bare branches of hedges shudder in the cold, their limbs knock against each other like chattering teeth. Fog hangs suspended in the air, as if a hand has reached up to pull down the clouds to cover the ground. Through the fog, a figure emerges, her slight shoulders hunched against the sudden gale. She carefully picks her way around the rocks scattered along the side of the road, careful to avoid the sloping ditch dug along its side. Her chestnut coloured hair floats around her narrow face.

It is early morning and the sky is grey. Dark rainclouds gather overhead and the world holds its breath while it awaits the downpour.

A bell chimes, the bright sound jarring in her ears, and Charlotte reaches into her pocket and withdraws her phone. The screen flashes, indicating that a call is waiting to be answered. She hits decline and tucks the phone back into her jacket. The wind tosses her hair into her eyes and she reaches up to push the hair away from her face. As she reaches up she bares the skin of her arm, a ring of olive bruises blossom on her pale skin like moss. She hurriedly pulls her sleeve down, even though there is no one around to see. The bruises faded from the violent purple shade they had been when she left home. It feels strange to her to look at the bruises and feel wistful for the time when she received them. They time before everything changed.

The wind dies down, and silence hangs heavily in the air. A crack of thunder sounds overhead and the sky bursts open. Rain pours down, soaking the road. Charlotte does not have an umbrella and there is no shelter to wait under. She resigns herself to the fact that no matter what she does she will be soaked so she continues on her way. Charlotte follows the twisting road back into town but she will not arrive for quite some time.

The rain stops as suddenly as it began. The landscape drenched in deep blacks and greens, greys and blue, all blurring together as Charlotte blinks the rainwater from her eyes. She hears a distant rumbling and looks over her shoulder to see a pair of glowing yellow eyes staring at her through the fog. No, not eyes. Headlights. They are coming closer, faster.

She hears the screeching sound of the tires skidding across the wet pavement before she sees the car. The black Lexus careens out of the fog and she leaps away from the road. Her heart is beating faster, harder, its fevered beats pulsing in her chest, the base of her throat, her temples. She gasps as the car spins down the road and veers sharply to the side, it speeds straight ahead and tears over the soft shoulder, driving headlong into the ditch that runs along its side, its rear end suspended uselessly in the air. A terrible, whining, grinding sound fills the air as the tires spin furiously.

 

She is frozen in place, terror grasps at her throat, each gasp of air more painful than the last. Then, as quickly as it came, the fear melts and she sprints over to the side of the road to peer into the ditch. Through the windows she can see a still figure in the driver's seat.

Carefully she treads down the slope of the ditch, rocks and grass tumbling in her wake. She picks her way through the shallow water that has gathered at the base of the ditch and approaches the driver's seat. She hesitates as she draws near. Gathering her courage she taps on the window. A pale face glares at her from within.

The door whips open and a gasping man falls out. Blood flows from a cut on his temple and runs down his face like a crimson tear. He looks at his car suspended in the air like some careless child has tossed it aside.

"Fuck!" His voice is snatched away by the wind. "Fuck!" He repeats, whirling around to face Charlotte.

"Are you okay?" She asks, eyeing his bloodied face with alarm.

"Do I *look* like I am okay? The *fuck* were you doing in the middle of the road?" He shouts.

She winces slightly but does not cower from his anger.

"I wasn't in the middle of the road, I was walking along the side," she answers calmly.

"What the bloody hell are you doing walking along the side of the road in this weather? No wonder my car's in the fucking ditch!"

"You've had an accident," she begins and he cuts her off with a sharp laugh.

"No fucking kidding!"

She swallows the rest of her sentence, acknowledging that he is in no state to listen to her and reaches into her pocket for her phone.

"Going to take a selfie?" He sneers.

She ignores him and dials 911.

A highway marker indicates their location and she reads it aloud to the dispatcher on the phone, she hopes they can her over the man's expletives.

After the dispatcher disconnects she drops her phone into her pocket and turns back to the man. He is sitting on the side of the road, his head in his hands. Hesitantly, Charlotte approaches and hovers beside him.

"Are you okay?"

He raises his head to give her an incredulous stare.

"Obviously not."

"I called 911—" she begins but he cuts her off with a dark laugh.

"911? What are they going to do? You should have called a fucking tow truck after you *wrecked my car*."

Charlotte does not shrink from his fury, if anything it makes her furious in turn. "I didn't do anything to your car, you're the one who drove it off the road. And if you want a tow, call it yourself. I called 911 because you seem to have lost a lot of blood. Would you like to wait for the ambulance on your own and possibly faint from blood loss? Because if you continue to speak to me like that I am going to leave you here."

As she speaks his mouth hangs open, his face devoid of expression. When she finishes his mouth snaps closed and his lips quirk in a grin.

     MEAGAN CLEVELAND

"I deserved that I suppose." He gestures to the stretch of road beside him. "By all means, wait with me. Make sure I don't die of blood loss."

Charlotte sighs and settles next to the man. "I said possibly faint from blood loss, not die."

"And what makes you such an expert?"

"My mom is a nurse."

He squints at her, the blood still trickling from the wound on his forehead obscuring his sight. "*She's* a nurse. Not you."

Charlotte frowns at him. "I'm just trying to help."

The man rolls his eyes. "So you keep saying." He mutters darkly. "Tell me," he begins, cocking his head to the side to assess her. "What are you doing out in the middle of nowhere on your own?" Charlotte glares at him and he raises his hands in mock defence. "I'm just curious."

"You sure?" Charlotte snaps in response. "Seems like you were trying to blame me for your poor driving skills again."

This startles a laugh out of the man, the sound echoing around them.

"No, not that. Really, what are you doing out here on your own? You're awfully far from town. Did you walk all this way?"

Charlotte nods. "I needed to clear my head."

"Bad day?" Charlotte nods again. "I understand what that's like," he says, gesturing to the car wreck behind him. This time, Charlotte is the one to laugh.

The sound of sirens rings faintly in the distance.

"Ah, they're on their way. Still think I'll die of blood loss before they get here?"

Charlotte raises her hand to her chin and appraises him. He laughs again. "I think you'll live."

"Do you mind staying with me anyway? The least they can do is give you a lift into town."

Charlotte agrees and remains seated on the side of the road next to the wounded man until the ambulance pulls up beside them. By that time the blood has stopped flooding down his face, instead it dries on his pasty skin like flakes of rust. The paramedics rush over and shine a light into his pupils. He begins to swear again.

"The pupils are dilated." One of the paramedics calls over to the other. "Possible head trauma."

The man waves a hand airily before his face, "Pfft. I'll be grand." He moves to rise to his feet and the paramedics rush to his side and help ease him upright.

"Careful, sir, you may have a concussion."

The paramedics wrangle him into the ambulance and Charlotte hovers nervously behind them. They are about to close the doors when the man throws out and arm and sits bolt upright.

"Wait!" He beckons for Charlotte to come closer. "She's coming with me. She needs a ride into town."

"We're sorry sir. This is an ambulance, not a taxi."

"Are you fucking kidding me? We've both been traumatized, you can't leave her here—"

"It's okay. I'll be fine." Charlotte says.

"You sure?" He appraises her with a frown.

"I'll be fine." Charlotte repeats.

"Alright. But don't go causing anymore accidents while I'm away. And," he begins to say as he pats down his torso and looks into his jacket, "If you're going to stay out here could you do me a favour? I wasn't messing about when I

 MEAGAN CLEVELAND

said I needed a tow. Can you call them for me? I'd call them myself but my phone is somewhere in there," he waves at the Lexus suspended in the air. Finally, he seems to find what he is looking for and digs deep in his pocket with a grin. "Here's my information, you can give it to them when they arrive," he whips his hand out of his pocket and hands her a business card. "Stay out of the fucking road—"

Losing their patience with their passenger, the paramedics shut the doors on him mid sentence. Charlotte watches the ambulance drive away and calls a tow truck. As she waits for them to arrive she turns the card over in her hands and almost drops it when she reads the name emblazoned on its front.

*Dr. Ellis O'Farrell, Professor, Art History*
*Thornfield Hall*

# CHAPTER FOUR

## REVERIE

Charlotte starts when the the tow truck arrives, as if starting awake from a dream. The sound of rattling wheels churning over rocks strewn about the country road draws her from her reverie. The driver agrees to give her a lift into town and she spends the bumpy ride staring fixedly at the card in her hand. She reaches into her pocket to draw out her phone, taking a photo of the details of the card. Soon they have rumbled into town and the driver drops her off at the university. Before she hops out she passes the card to the driver and instructs him to call the number at the bottom when the car is ready to be picked up. She stands by the side of the road, newly fallen leaves skittering across her feet, and watches the truck rumble off, dragging the wreck of the Lexus in its wake.

She wanders home, oblivious to the people going about their day around her, her mind elsewhere.

Dr. Ellis O'Farrell. So *that* is the man she would be working with. She now understands Joanna's words at the luncheon. He is a difficult man, but nothing she couldn't handle. The anxiety of the unknown faded once she felt that spark of recognition upon reading his name.

Charlotte lived her whole life with difficult people. She knows that the way to deal with them is to quietly anticipate what they want before they storm and rage for it. Her life has been spent avoiding storms, preparing for the worst. But, being on guard constantly is exhausting. The thought of one more conflict to deal with gave her a panic attack at the luncheon, fearing that she would have to guard herself against Dr. O' Farrell on top of everything else. But after their encounter this afternoon, she knows she has what it takes to stand up to him.

She is smiling when she makes her way up the stairs of her building and into her apartment.

The next morning, Charlotte settles herself at her desk in the graduate office, stack of postcards and prints ready to decorate her desk. She hums happily as she pins up postcards of her favourite paintings: Goya's *The Third of May 1808*, Gericault's *Raft of the Medusa*, David's *Oath of the Horatii*, and Fuseli's *The Nightmare*. In between the postcards she pins up her own drawings done in charcoal: a profile of her grandmother, a sketch of a hyacinth, and a study of Delacroix's *Liberty Leading the People*.

Adele makes her way into the office and stops short behind her, admiring her handwork.

"Nice." She says approvingly.

"Thanks." Charlotte smiles over her shoulder at the other girl. They chat for a few minutes before respectively turning to their laptops.

Charlotte logs into her campus email and scrolls through the slog of information about orientation week events and emails from the graduate student union but there is a name she recognizes. Her heart halts for a moment as she spots the email from Dr. O' Farrell.

**Dear Charlotte,**

**As you may have heard from my colleagues at the graduate luncheon, I was not due back in town until next week. However, I have come back a little early and would like to set up a meeting before our first class next Wednesday. Please let me know when you are available.**

**Cheers,**

**Dr. Ellis O'Farrell Phd**

Charlotte stares at the email for a moment. She did not think she would see him again so soon. He must not have stayed at the hospital very long. She spins in her chair to face her office mate.

"Adele," Adele looks up from her screen and spins around to face her. "Do you know where Dr. O' Farrell's office is?"

Adele frowns. "I do. But Dr. Fairfax said he isn't supposed to be in town until next week."

"He isn't supposed to be. He got back early and wants to meet."

Understanding dawns on Adele's face. "I get it. You want to drop in and introduce yourself before the big scary meeting?"

Charlotte shrugs. "I might as well take a look and see if he is here, and introduce myself now."

"Good idea! Shows initiative. His office is down the hall, past the conference room to the left. I can show you if you'd like me to." Adele offers, rising from her chair.

"No. No need, I can find it." Charlotte assures her, not wanting an audience to her reunion with the unpleasant man. She predicts that Adele will be able to hear his swearing from their office anyway. "Thanks."

Charlotte shuts her laptop with a soft *snap*, and pushes away from the desk. She walks leisurely down the hall and on the way runs into Dr. Fairfax.

"Hi Cat," she greets the older woman. Today her bright orange hair is set in pin curls that frame her angular face and she wears a string of pearls with her twinset and slacks.

"Good morning!" She smiles. "You'll never believe who's here! Ellis, that is, Dr. O' Farrell, has come back from his conference early." She leans in and utters quietly, "and it looks like he's had a rough time of it too. He's in the last office on the left if you want to pop in and say hello."

"I will." Charlotte bids goodbye to her advisor and continues on her way down the hall. The door is half open, a thin sliver of bright morning light slicing across the floor. Charlotte hesitates by the doorway. Steeling herself she inhales slowly and raises her hand to the door, rapping it with her knuckles.

"Come in," a muffled voice calls from within.

Charlotte pushes the door open.

She takes a look inside the office and blinks. Every available surface in the office is covered. The bookshelves are bursting with books, books sit in piles upon the floor, the chair facing the desk, and on the desk itself. In between piles of books, towers of paper tremble and threaten to spill onto the floor. The fence of books and paper obscures the figure sitting at the desk behind them.

"Dr. O' Farrell?"

An impatient sigh dangerously shifts the piles of paper, a single sheet gently soars onto the floor to land at Charlotte's feet.

Charlotte gets a brief glimpse of him. His skin is pale, his eyes ringed black from tiredness. A white bandage is stuck to his high forehead, a faint red smear showing through the layers of gauze.

He glances up to peer at her from around the stack of papers, and recognition sparks in his eyes. He leaps from his chair and the papers go flying. The sheets of paper dance around them like a whirlwind but their eyes are locked on each other.

"It's you." He says. "My would be murderer."

Charlotte frowns. "I thought we settled that yesterday. It was an accident."

"Sure it was. Have you come to finish the job?"

She shakes her head in reply, too exasperated for words. She bends forward to gather the papers strewn at her feet.

"Ah, just leave it, leave it." He starts forward and reaches for the paper, his hand touching hers. She pauses for a moment, her eyes flashing towards his, then looking away. She shoves the papers into his waiting hands. She is dismayed to see him toss the papers carelessly over his shoulder. "I'm surprised you came to see me. Is it something to do with the car?"

She shakes her head again, glancing at the chair. He follows her gaze and leaps forward to shove the books from

          MEAGAN CLEVELAND

the seat and onto the floor. Stepping back he gestures grandly to the vacated chair.

"Please, sit."

Charlotte tiptoes around the fallen books, avoiding a cracked spine here, a hardback there, and settles in the chair. Dr. O' Farrell pushes the papers back from the corner of the desk and perches there. He looks at her expectantly.

"Is it about the car?" He repeats.

"No. It has nothing to do with that actually. You sent me an email."

He frowns.

"I did? Sorry, but I have no idea who you are."

Charlotte glowers at him.

"I'm your teaching assistant."

He raises his eyebrows. "Are you now? Is that why you were trying to kill me before term starts?"

"For god's sake." Charlotte mutters darkly, rising from the chair and tripping over books in her haste to get to the door. "I had no idea who you were until you handed me your card. When I got your email I wondered whether you might be in the building and thought I would come and introduce myself properly."

She watches impassively as he straightens and walks purposefully over the mounds of paper to stop before her and extend his hand.

"Ellis O'Farrell."

Charlotte stares at the proffered hand for a moment before returning the gesture. Soon her small hand is clasped in his. She is surprised at the callouses she can feel on his fingertips as they brush against her palm.

"Charlotte. Charlotte Grey."

"Well Charlotte Grey, I'd say it was nice to meet you, but seeing as I barely escaped our first meeting with my life—" he stops with a grin. "I know, I know, I'm not one to give up a joke. I'm glad you've come to introduce yourself. I was wondering who the crazy woman on the side of the road was." As he jokes, he continues to hold her hand in his. Seeming to realize this he drops it quickly and steps back, rubbing his hands together. "So, let's talk art!"

# CHAPTER FIVE

## LUDUM

Charlotte feels as if she gets to know Dr. O' Farrell quite quickly.

Joanna is wrong. He isn't a difficult man, or a cruel one. He is impulsive, he says whatever first comes into his head without thinking of the ramifications later on. A dangerous habit for an academic. But he isn't cruel. He is kind, in his own peculiar way.

They spend that first afternoon talking about art while the rays of afternoon sun shift along the walls of his office until that last great flare of sunset blazes through the windows, glaring into their eyes. Even then they don't stop talking, instead, they move to another location, the Grad Lounge, a pub on campus for faculty and graduate students to meet in a more relaxed setting. Dr. O' Farrell grabs two drinks and they talk until Charlotte has to give in and go home to bed. She smiles the whole way home.

That week she would habitually drop into his office for a chat, discussing art and history, and whatever else they are most interested in. It is Friday now, and Charlotte begins the now familiar trek down the hall to his office only to stand, confused, before a closed door.

He kept the door open all week, how strange that he should close it now. Perhaps he isn't in today. Perhaps he needed to get some work done. Begrudgingly, Charlotte turns from that closed door and drifts back to her office. She reaches for the assigned text for the course she is assisting for and begins the readings for their first class on Monday, jotting down notes in her leather notebook. Soon she is lost in the reading, her mind flooded with images of Christ and the Virgin Mary depicted in oil and charcoal by master painters. Her eyes dance from the text to her notebook and she starts. She stares at the pen in her hand, and the drawing of a hand she sketched in the margins. A hand reaching out, an x-acto knife discarded beside it. As she stares at the sketch, the memory of that night overlaps with reality and blood rushes to her head, making her dizzy. She inhales sharply, holding the breath then exhaling in a rush, gripping the pen hard in her hand, she scribbles over the sketch until the paper tears.

After she is finished her readings she goes home for the night to her small, lonely, apartment. She is currently living in the apartments offered only to graduate students, a building that promises quiet, set apart from the frenzied partying of the undergrads.

The rooms have a small living area and kitchenette, a bathroom and bedroom. Basic furnishings are included but Charlotte brought a few of her own things to make the rooms more like home. A brightly coloured blanket drapes over white sheets, colourful illustrations of flowers are framed and hang on white walls. These touches made to personalize the place simply make her feel like a guest in this new place.

     

Charlotte grabbed takeout on her way home, and gently places the dish in the microwave to warm up. The hum of the microwave is the only sound in that empty place. When she first arrived she thought the rooms were huge, so much more space than her tiny bedroom at home. But now, strangely, the rooms seem smaller without the bustling presence of her family. The microwave stops with a shrill beep and then goes silent.

The silence is deafening.

Charlotte spent her whole life shouting for her brother to just be quiet, to just leave her alone, and now, finally finding the quiet she craved she desperately wishes for the silence to be filled with the noise of sharing a space with another person. Silence reminds her how alone she is.

Wiping away the tear that falls down her cheek, Charlotte brusquely grabs the dish from the microwave and sits at the small table. The food is delicious but sits heavily in her stomach. Each bite becomes harder and harder to swallow, a lump forming in her throat. Tears begin to stream down her cheeks. She does not wipe them away but continues eating.

She curls up on her bed, drawing the vibrant red blanket under her arms, and closes her eyes. She waits for Monday to come.

When Monday dawns Charlotte feels like a different person. Hope flutters in the pit of her stomach. She would see him today.

She spends her morning doing research for her thesis. She does not go to his office that afternoon, fearing that closed door and how the sight of it would make her feel. She keeps her mind busy until it is time for their first class together.

Last week Dr. O' Farrell had given her a set of keys and instructions on how to set the class up before the lecture would start. She leaves the office and heads for the classroom far earlier then she needed to, but she is anxious to have everything just right for when he arrives.

She goes up the stairs to the main floor of the building. The lecture hall is locked, but she has the key. She opens the doors and begins setting up. She presses on a series of switches and glowing buttons until the lecture hall lights up and an enormous screen slowly lowers itself behind her. While she works students begin to trickle in, groups of students laughing and smiling together, soon the cavernous space resounds with the clamour of so many young people. Charlotte feels a pang of jealousy, seeing so many friends sitting together, and she pushes the jealousy down. Everything is set up and ready to go, with minutes to spare. She turns from the front of the room and sits in one of the vacant seats.

The students fall silent as the door bursts open and slams shut in quick succession.

Professor O'Farrell has arrived.

He hurries through the doorway, head down. Slinging his bag off his shoulder he glances up to check that the AV equipment is set up. He nods curtly towards Charlotte and she hates the small burst of pride his acknowledgement gives her.

He takes out his notes slowly, arranges them on his desk and fishes a microphone from his pocket and clips it onto the

     **MEAGAN CLEVELAND**

lapel of his blazer. He steps up to the podium, makes a show of straightening his notes. Finally, he looks up at the class.

He has their complete attention.

"How many of you," he begins slowly, taking his papers and laying them facedown and stepping away from the podium to address the class. "How many of you are here because of the DaVinci Code?"

Charlotte suppresses a laugh at the question. She knows where this is going.

Hands shoot up like flowers in spring.

"That's quite a few hands. Did you watch the film as kids and decide you wanted to become a symbologist like Robert Langdon?" Heads nod in unison. A few nervous laughs titter in the crowd.

A smile tugs at the corner of Professor O'Farrel's lips. It is not a pleasant smile. More of a sneer if anything.

"I hate to tell you this. But there is no such thing as a symbologist."

Silence cuts through the room like a blade.

Professor O'Farrell turns back to the podium. An image appears behind him, its vibrant colours dance across his face and for a moment he appears to be a saint made of stained glass, a halo of colour glowing around his head.

"There is no such thing as a symbologist," he pauses and looks around the room, "but the importance of symbols in art cannot be denied."

He steps aside so the class can take in the image floating behind him. It is Raphael's *School of Athens*. Taking his laser pointer, he fixes its red light on each figure and identifies them, explaining who they represent in the School of Athens and their contemporary counterpart in the life of the artist. Charlotte looks around at the rapt faces of the students and smiles.

The class is done all too soon. Charlotte quickly gathers her things together, hoping to walk back to her office with Dr. O' Farrell. But a ring of undergraduates separates her from the professor, and she patiently stands by her chair, waiting for an opening. Soon the students trickle away and hope flutters inside her again only to die when she sees the empty space by the podium.

He has left without her.

# CHAPTER SIX

## AD MELIORA

**B**lood rushes in her ears.

He left without her.

She feels the hot flood of tears well in her eyes but blinks the tears away, wiping furiously at her cheeks.

He left without her.

She stalks out of the classroom and stomps down the stairs back to her office, all the while cursing herself.

Idiot. She is a complete and utter idiot. He is a professor, she has deluded herself into thinking that he is her friend. She is so ridiculously lonely she thinks the man she is essentially working for is her friend.

She bursts through the doors to the ground floor and stomps down the hallway, eyes fixed ahead. She refuses to look at his office. She holds her breath as she storms by, eyes fixed straight ahead, when the closed office door bursts open.

"What, were you going to walk by and not say hello?" He says.

Charlotte stands and gapes at him for a moment. Then she pushes past him into the office, hands clenched into fists.

Inhale. Hold. Exhale.

Charlotte repeats this process several times before she is calm enough to speak. Her hands are clenched into fists, her fingernails leaving red crescents in her palms.

He must sense that she is upset because for once he is silent. He does not offer a clever quip, a tired joke or interesting fact. He simply holds his tongue and watches her expectantly, waiting for her to speak.

Finally, words are able to form through the red mist that has descended on her mind.

"You left without me." He opens his mouth to speak and she holds up a hand. "Please, let me finish. You left without me after class. And when I went by your office this morning the door was closed. I got the sense that you wanted to be alone."

"Don't be daft. You've got it wrong—" he begins to protest. Again she holds up a hand and he falls silent.

"You are right. I did get it wrong. I let myself think that I had made a friend. But this," she gestures to the space in between them. "This isn't friendship. I'm not your friend. I *work* for you. There is an imbalance of power here. I take my cues from you. When I saw the closed door I took that to mean you didn't need me hanging around."

She avoided looking at him while she spoke. Now, her eyes drift to his face. His brow is furrowed, a frown twists his lips. He, on the other hand, does not avoid her gaze, he stares at her with an intensity that brings heat to her cheeks.

"You're wrong." She stiffens at the words but he does not relent. "You are wrong. We are friends, you and I. I apologize for giving you the wrong impression this morning. I wasn't ignoring you, I wasn't actually here yet. I barely made it in time for class actually. I had an appointment run longer than

I anticipated. And after class I had a call I needed to make. It was rude of me not to say hello. Forgive me?"

Charlotte simply stares at him. She didn't think of the possibility that he might be late. She must look like an idiot for making a scene.

She nods curtly and a smile brightens his face.

"What did you think of the lecture?"

She is relieved at the change in subject.

"I enjoyed it. It seemed like the students did too."

He grins. "They do enjoy a show."

They chat for a little while longer when a phone begins to ring. He fishes in his pocket and withdraws a cell phone. He squints at the screen and sighs.

"Finally, she calls me back." He rolls his eyes. "Sorry I've got to take this. Mother-in-law."

The words feel like a blow. Her eyes dart to his finger. She doesn't see a ring.

"You have a wife?" The words tumble from her lips, unbidden.

Now he does avoid her gaze. "Not anymore."

He put the phone to his ear and Charlotte eases out of the door.

Back in the office, Adele sits at her desk typing up a proposal for a paper. Charlotte sags into the chair next to her. Adele pulls the earbuds from her ears and gives her a sympathetic look.

"Rough day?"

"Is Dr. O' Farrell married?" Again the words pour out of her unbidden.

Adele raises an eyebrow.

"I don't mean it like that." She protests, the unspoken question hanging in the air between them.

"If you say so." She laughs at the pained expression on Charlotte's face. "Okay, okay. Yes he was married, but his wife died years ago. Brain cancer."

"Oh my god. That's terrible."

Adele nods. "It is. They got married in grad school. They discovered the tumour too late for treatment. But it's been years. He's had flings with other professors on campus. He is kinda notorious for it really." The brow arches again. "Why do you ask?"

"I was just chatting with him when he said he got a call from his mother-in-law."

"Yeah, he is still really close to her. He brings her as his plus one to department parties."

"Really?"

"Yeah, Antoinette was her only daughter so Dr. O' Farrell is all she has left."

"That's kind of sweet that he spends so much time with her."

"I don't know, they aren't the nicest to each other. I get the sense they don't like each other very much. But they continue to spend time together because of who they have in common. Like, if they remember her together it's as if she isn't gone."

"How do you know so much about it?" Charlotte asks suspiciously. "You can't know that much just from doing your undergrad here."

"Oh, well, um, it's probably because he used to date my sister."

"What?" Charlotte gasps.

"Calm down!" Adele laughs. "It was when my sister was doing her PhD. It didn't last too long, barely a year. But I got to know him a bit and then I started my undergrad and took some classes with him after they broke up. It was weird at first but he's such a great lecturer I forgot how he drove my sister crazy."

"So he dated other professors and grad students?" Charlotte muses aloud.

Adele frowns. "Don't get any ideas. He is a great lecturer and a brilliant scholar. But you don't want to get tied up with him. Believe me."

# CHAPTER SEVEN

## AUXILIUM

Charlotte does not heed Adele's warning.

Over the course of several weeks, Professor O'Farrell becomes as familiar to her as her own self. She finds her heart beats faster the closer she comes to his office. She learns to recognize the soft tread of his feet upon the creaking floorboards, the whisper of his sigh as they mark quizzes together, the gentle touch of his fingertips as their hands meet over a stack of exams, the touch sending her heart racing. She replays these moments to herself as she falls asleep at night to distract from the recurring image of bloodied bandages flashing in her mind every time she closes her eyes. But when guilt gnaws away the happy memories of her time spent with the professor she rises from her bed and reaches for her sketch book. She sketches out the distressing images that bombard her, trapping the image on paper so that she can shut the image away. Once the pages are crammed with crowded sketches of bandaged wrists, discarded x-acto knives, of clenched fists, and brows drawn low over familiar dark eyes only then do her eyelids begin to droop and her shoulders sag and finally she plunges into dreamless sleep.

She hopes that her work will keep her busy enough to keep the images at bay. For a time it works, engrossing herself so deeply in her studies that by day her mind is blissfully clear and she prepares herself to face the onslaught of images that would come each night. But soon her plan fails. One early October afternoon she sits in a seminar listening to a classmate's presentation when her sight narrows and the image of a pale hand flashes in her mind, its fingers limp and listless, dark blood puddled beneath the wrist. She inhales sharply and heads turn her way. She feigns a cough and reaches for her water bottle and takes a sip to mask her distress. She ceases listening to the presentation and brandishes her pen like a shield. Once the pen hits paper, the familiar strokes ease her tense shoulders and she begins to breathe again. The presentation finishes and Charlotte looks down in horror to see that same listless hand on the margins of the presentation handout. She scribbles her pen over the drawing so fiercely that the paper begins to tear. The rest of the class begins to pack up around her and she shoves the handout into her notebook, tucking them both away into her satchel. She starts to bring the sketchbook to campus. When the flashes start she reaches for its familiar weight and feels calm descend. She knows now not to commit pen to paper while she is in public, and instead sketches out the flashes with her fingertip atop the table.

One sunny October afternoon, Charlotte is flooded with images of that pale hand while having a meeting with Dr. O' Farrell. As soon as her vision begins to narrow and that hand flashes in her mind she shuts her eyes and inhales slowly, desperately trying not to attract his attention. She opens an eye to see that he is quite engrossed with his own words, leaning back in his chair, feet up on the corner of his desk, he gesticulates wildly as he talks, certain that her attention is on him. But his words fall on deaf ears, blood rushes in her ears and all she can hear is a shrill sound, like the shriek of a kettle once the water has boiled. She reaches for the familiar weight of her sketchbook at her side, clenching the book tightly in her hands. Her eyes must have drifted shut. She opens them to see the professor staring at her.

"You alright?" He asks, a frown marring his face.

"Yes," She gasps, finding it hard to draw air.

"Hey, hey," He straightens quickly, his feet thudding to the floor. He fumbles around on his desk, grabs a mug and pushes it towards her. "Here, have this. I just made it but I haven't touched it."

She reaches for the mug, fingertips brushing against his, but she doesn't even feel it, a heaviness has settled on her chest and each breath feels like it is being drawn through mud. She lifts the mug with shaking hands and drinks, spluttering as she struggles to drink and breathe at the same time.

Warm hands settle on her shoulders. "Don't choke, I'd hate to find another teaching assistant now."

She suppresses a laugh and begins to cough, the sketchbook falling to the floor with a dull thump.

Professor O'Farrell reaches down and picks up the sketchbook, its pages fluttering open, the familiar hand waving bleakly at them from its pages. His frown deepens when he sees the first sketch of that hand. He flicks through

 MEAGAN CLEVELAND

the pages, a crease appearing on his brow as he sees how the image repeats on each page.

"What is this?" He asks quietly, she can barely hear his voice over the rasp of the pages against his fingertips.

"That's private." She manages to say hoarsely, reaching out for the sketchbook. He does not notice the gesture. He is staring at the sketches of limp hands, bandaged wrists and accusing eyes. His own eyes flicker towards her wrists and she feels outrage churn in her stomach.

"It's not my hand, it's not my wrists." She defends herself.

"Whose are they?" He demands.

She rises from the chair and yanks the sketchbook from his grasp, holding it close to her chest.

"My brother's."

"Did something happen to him?" Though he asks the question, she can see from his face that he knows the answer.

"My brother didn't want me to go to school here. He didn't want me to move so far away. He told me I couldn't go. I told him it wasn't his decision to make. So he cut his wrists the night before I was supposed to move here."

"Jesus." He runs a hand through his dark hair. "Are you okay?"

"I'm fine." She replies, a little too loudly.

He stares at her face for some time, then looks at the book.

"Of course you are."

She turns and leaves his office.

Things become strained between them after that. She feels his pitying glances and hears his soft tones and begins to resent him for it. The images begin to flood her so often now the sketchbook is soon filled and she needs to go out and get a new one.

After one long, restless night, she arrives on campus with dark circles under her eyes. She sits, silent, in his office as he tells her the plan for that week, his voice barely getting through. After the deep rumble of his voice has ceased she looks up to find him staring at her.

Dr. O' Farrell rises from his chair. "I need to talk to you." He gestures weakly at the door behind her. "Would you mind closing that?"

Worried now, she turns to close the door with a soft click. Dr. O' Farrell pulls over his chair from behind his desk and brings it closer to her. He sits and stares at her.

"Is everything okay?" She asks.

Dr. O' Farrell takes in a breath. "I'm not so sure."

"Is there anything I can do to help you?"

He shakes his head. "It's not me I'm worried about. It's you."

She draws back. "What about me?"

"Things seem...off lately. I noticed you aren't eating during our meetings like you used to. You don't seem very happy."

"I'm not." She replies softly.

He nods. "I thought so." He rolls his chair closer to hers, their knees almost touching. "Will you come somewhere with me?"

"Okay."

He nods again and stands. She stands with him. He takes her chair back to its desk and holds the door open for her. Silently they walk down the hall, up the stairs and outside. It is warm for October and they don't need to grab their

    MEAGAN CLEVELAND

jackets. Every so often Dr. O' Farrell will turn and smile her way and indicate with his head where they are headed. Soon she realizes where they were going.

She stops.

"The counsellor? I don't need counselling." She folds her arms across her chest.

Dr. O' Farrell turns to face her and looks her in the eyes. "I think you do. Look," He runs a hand through his hair and draws in a deep breath and looks away. "It will help. It helps me anyway."

"You've been to counselling?"

His eyes go back to her face. His hand drops to his sides. "Yeah. Just try it and see?"

It is the hopeful look on his face that does it. With a groan she continues walking. He falls in step beside her. Reaching out he places a hand on her shoulder briefly, his hand warm and reassuring. Then his hand drops to his side again. They walk into the building together and he goes over to the desk with her to ask to speak to someone. And now, here they are. Sitting together in the drab grey office on the uncomfortable grey chairs, a clipboard balanced on her knees, and on that clipboard is a questionnaire.

**Please rate your mood based on how you've been feeling in the last two weeks. 1 being extremely poor, 10 being extremely good.**

If she is being honest, she would circle 1 or 2. But to be safe she settles on an 5.

Over the last two weeks have you been bothered by any of the following problems?

**Little interest or pleasure in doing things**

1   2   3   4   5   6   7   8   9   10

**Feeling down, depressed, or hopeless**

1   2   3   4   5   6   7   8   9   10

**Felling tired or having little energy**

1   2   3   4   5   6   7   8   9   10

**Poor appetite or overeating**

1   2   3   4   5   6   7   8   9   10

She circles 5 for each question. Lately she has very little interest in doing anything. She has been waking up every morning and vomiting bile. She hasn't eaten breakfast in weeks and finds she has to remind herself to eat throughout the day to prevent herself from getting headaches. Admittedly, things have felt a little hopeless. The sketchbook helped at first, but now she is on her way to fill a second sketchbook things seem bleaker than ever.

She finishes the questionnaire and stands to hand it over to the receptionist. She turns from the desk to look at the man she came in with. He has his copy of the course textbook open across his lap, reading its contents with a frown. He must have felt her eyes on him for he glances over at her to offer a small smile. She looks away.

          MEAGAN CLEVELAND

"Charlotte Grey?" A voice calls out.

Dr. O' Farrell smiles encouragingly at her as she joins the counsellor and follows her to her office. She glances over her shoulder before she enters the room, his smile the last thing she sees before the door closes between them.

# CHAPTER EIGHT

## RUBRUM

"So, Charlotte, what brings you in today?" The counsellor asks as she takes a seat behind her desk. Charlotte perches on the edge of a small chair facing directly across from her, a small table with a box of tissues is positioned beside her. Charlotte resolves that she will not use them.

"Someone I work with brought me in." Charlotte replies quietly.

"They brought you in? You didn't come in on your own?" Charlotte shakes her head.

"I see. So, you don't think there is anything wrong." The sentence is not a question. Again, Charlotte shakes her head.

"I didn't say that." Charlotte looks down at her hands in her lap. "I know something is wrong, but I am trying not to let it affect me. If I work hard enough, keep myself busy enough, I can keep it all out of my mind."

"Some coping mechanisms end up making the problem you are trying to run from worse." The counsellor replies, her eyes fixed on Charlotte. Charlotte glances away from her face to focus on the art hanging on the wall behind her. A print of Matisse's *The Dessert: Harmony in Red*. The painting depicts a woman in a black dress laying a table, the tablecloth and the walls behind painted in a vivid red. Charlotte frowns. Red is not a particularly calming colour, if she had chosen a painting for a counsellor's office she would have chosen something by Monet in calming blues and greens and violets. Not red.

"Distracted?" The counsellor quips. Charlotte glances away from the painting to see a bemused expression on the counsellor's face.

"I am a graduate student studying art history. I was just looking at your painting."

The counsellor turns in her chair to look up at the painting above her, then turns back to Charlotte. "The painting came with the office."

"I was just thinking it was a strange choice to put in a room for people in crisis to come to. I would have thought you would have chosen something in more calming colours."

"Again, the painting came with the room I'm afraid. Is there anything particularly offensive you find with it? Just looks like a woman getting ready for dinner to me."

"It's the vibrant reds, the bold brushstrokes. It's very in your face."

"It is a lot of red. The colour of passion."

"And blood." The words escape just as quickly as Charlotte thinks them. She inhales sharply and the counsellor straightens in her chair.

"That's an interesting connection. Have you experienced anything traumatic recently?"

Charlotte bristles at the question. Of course she's experienced something traumatic, why else would she be seeing a crisis counsellor? What a stupid question.

For a moment she wants to refuse answering. She wants to get up and storm out of the room, out of the building, and go home and hide under the covers. Instead she meets the counsellor's eager gaze. She might as well tell the truth.

"My family didn't want me to move away and come to school here. My mother thinks graduate school is a waste of time and money. And my brother," she inhales sharply again before moving on, "my brother thought I was abandoning him. The day before I left we had a big argument about it. He didn't want me to go and he went into my room and dumped out all the boxes I had packed. I was so angry at him. I said some things I didn't mean, and I left. I spent the day at the library and didn't come home until much, much later. I went to sleep, I had to get up early to make the drive here, but I was woken up by a scream. I followed the screams to my brother's room. My mom was standing in the way, screaming. I pushed past her and there he was, lying on the floor." Charlotte looked over at the painting again, at the vibrant red. "There was blood everywhere. He had cut his wrists."

"You blame yourself." The counsellor observes.

"Obviously." Charlotte snaps. "He did it to get my attention, to show me I was the one to blame. I know it isn't my fault. But how would you feel if your sibling tried to commit suicide before you made a big life change?"

"Tried to commit suicide? He survived?"

"Yes, the EMTS got there in time to stop the bleeding. He was committed and has been under psychiatric care."

"Have you spoken to him since?"

Charlotte shakes her head. "No. But he calls me almost every day, the same time each day. And when it isn't him

 **MEAGAN CLEVELAND**

calling, it's my mother. She calls me over and over, leaves messages telling me what a bad daughter I am, what a bad sister, to have abandoned them like this."

"Have you ever picked up the phone?"

"No."

"Are they still calling you?"

"Not as often."

"Maybe you should give them a call. Then it will be on your terms. You may not be with them right now, but the incident was just as traumatic for you as it was for them. And here you are, in a new place, with new responsibilities. Graduate school is hard enough without having a family crisis on top of everything. You have composed yourself well, but it must be taking a strain if you've come to see me."

Charlotte stares at her for a moment before replying.

"I keep replaying that night in my mind. I see my brother, laying on the floor, the carpet stained with blood, his hand reaching out for me. I see it when I try to go to sleep at night, when I am in class, sometimes when I am having a conversation with someone. I don't know how to get it to stop."

The counsellor sets down her notebook and leans forward. "Charlotte, what happened to your brother is not your fault. But your subconscious *thinks* it is. You are racked with guilt for what happened, and for your response to it." She holds up a hand when Charlotte starts to splutter. "There is no proper way to respond to trauma, I'm not saying you did the wrong thing by carrying on and coming here. But, by moving here and avoiding speaking to your family, you haven't had a chance to get any closure. You keep reliving that incident because it was your last interaction with your family. If you reach out to them, give them a call, you'll see that that moment isn't suspended in time. You don't have to relive it. It is over. You need to come to terms with how to move on now that it has happened."

"How?"

"I can't tell you that. But I think if you reach out to your family and have the conversation that you have been avoiding you will find out how to move on yourself."

Charlotte leaves the appointment feeling a little numb. Dr. O' Farrell is sitting with his head thrown back, his eyes closed. When she comes to a halt beside his chair he opens an eye, spots her, and straightens in his chair.

"All done?"

She nods.

He rises and they make their way out of the building in utter silence.

Only once they are out in the open, the fall air crisp and cold around them, does he speak.

"How did it go?"

"She thinks I am avoiding my problems."

"Aren't you though?" Charlotte glares at him in response and he raises his hands in defence. "Sorry, it's not really my area of expertise. Hence why I brought you to an expert."

Charlotte pauses and turns to him. He takes a step back at the expression on her face.

"You okay?"

She shakes her head. "Not really. But, thank you. Thank you for seeing me as someone worth getting to know, thank you for noticing that something was off and trying to help. As annoyed as I am at you for butting in, I'm also touched that you cared enough to try to help."

He listens to her in silence, running a hand through his hair.

"Don't be daft. I'd do it for anyone."

She smiles in reply and they head back to Thornfield Hall together.

# CHAPTER NINE

## VOCATUM

Charlotte is staring at the phone in her hand. She only has to move her thumb, to select her mother's name from her contact list. But she doesn't. She sets the phone down and edits a paper she plans to submit to a conference being held at their department that semester. The paper explores the affect of trauma on artists and how capturing moments of trauma in paint can often be a cathartic experience. She soon loses herself to her work and the hours pass without notice.

An irritating buzzing breaks her focus. She glances to the bookshelf alongside her desk, where she placed her phone face down hours before. She grabs for it and looks down at the familiar number flashing there. The same number that calls the same time each day since she left home. Since the incident.

*You keep reliving that incident because it was your last interaction with your family. If you reach out to them, give them a call, you'll see that that moment isn't suspended in time.*

As much as she didn't want to hear it, the counsellor spoke the truth. Charlotte feels as if she has been suspended in time since that night, like a mosquito trapped in amber, doomed to be frozen at one of the worst moments of its life. These last few weeks she has felt trapped, as if her arms, her legs, are caught in some viscous fluid weighing her down. Each day the fluid starts to solidify and it becomes harder and harder to move, to live.

Charlotte does not want to be trapped any longer.

She accepts the call.

"Hello?" She says the word so quietly she is not sure he hears.

"Charlotte?" A familiar voice asks incredulously.

"Hey Geoffrey." She feels the hot flood of tears spill over her cheeks.

There is a beat of silence on the other line. Then a torrent of words.

"Hey! I'm so glad you picked up. All this time I thought you were angry with me. My therapist says anger can be a common response, and that I just needed to give you time, you know? She also said you might not be angry at all, that I might just be projecting my own feelings, and that you were just busy with grad school. So, have you been busy?"

Charlotte knows from the cadence of his voice, the speed at which he speaks, that he is having a good day.

"Yeah, I've been really busy with coursework and my teaching assignment. I'm learning a lot, and getting a lot of research done for my thesis."

"That's good." He falls silent for a moment. The cadence of his voice changes. "Were you angry?"

"Yes." She replies.

"At me?"

"Yes, I was. I was angry that you would do that to try to change my mind. That's why I wouldn't pick up. I was angry at you, at mom. Then I was angry at myself for thinking that, it wasn't about me at all was it? What you did was a cry for help. Instead of helping I abandoned you." Her voice breaks on the last word.

The silence between them is charged with all the feelings they haven't been able to share with each other. Somehow it is easier to tell the truth when she doesn't have to look at him, to see the scars on his wrists, the hurt in his eyes.

"It did feel like you abandoned me." The words feel like a blow. "But, I've talked about it with my therapist. She made me see it from your point of view. You've been taking care of me for years while mom worked so much, you were as much of a mother to me as she was. What I didn't see was that you are only a few years older than me, you aren't my mother, you're my sister. You deserved to have a life without me holding you back."

"You're not holding me back."

"I'm not now. But I was. I knew it too. I wanted to keep you to myself."

"I know." She sighs, wiping at the tears furiously. "I felt like I was forced to grow up too quickly, but at the same time I wasn't able to grow, to leave and find out who I was."

"Have you found out who you are now?"

"Not yet, but I think I am getting there."

Charlotte and Geoff talk until his time runs out. As good as it feels to finally talk to him, to finally know that he is okay, that he got through the worst and would heal, she worries that they will fall into their old routine. She establishes boundaries. She can't talk to him every day but they can talk once a week.

That night when she lays in her bed and waits for sleep to descend, there are no images floating in her mind's eye. Only peace.

The days pass by and Charlotte finds she is better equipped to handle everything now she has confronted her fears. She is glad that she picked up Geoff's call. But her mother has not picked up hers.

Autumn gilds the leaves gold and copper and they fall from the trees to scatter across the ground. Thanksgiving is quickly approaching and Charlotte decides it is time to go home.

She is on her way to Dr. O' Farrell's office, a stack of exams in her arms. She has just printed them off and everything is set for the midterm for their class the next day.

She enters his office and sets the stack of exams on a clear space on his desk. He looks up at her with a grin.

"Thanks for printing those off. So, game plan for tomorrow is to get to the exam hall early and to set them out on the desks before we let the students in. After we have collected them all we'll alphabetize them, and then divide them back in my office."

"Actually, I need to talk to you about that." Charlotte begins.

"What, do you have a preference for which exams you'd like to mark?"

"No. I'll be able to collect the exams and bring them to your office afterward but I can't stay. I have to catch the train."

"Catch the train." He repeats flatly.

"Yes, catch the train home. For Thanksgiving."

His eyebrows raise.

"That's this week?"

"Yes."

"And you're going to go home to be with your mother? I thought you two weren't talking."

"She hasn't picked up when I've tried to call, but I texted her to let her know I am coming home and she acknowledged that."

"Sounds awful."

Charlotte shrugged.

"It's okay. I'm going to see my brother as well."

Dr. O' Farrell's face clouds with confusion. "You mean his grave?"

"Grave?" Charlotte repeats, puzzled.

"Didn't he kill himself?'

"No! He tried to kill himself. My mother had him committed afterward. He is in a psychiatric hospital."

Dr. O' Farrell raises his eyebrows. "That's terrible."

"It was terrible to find him, and have to leave afterward. I've been avoiding his calls. But I finally reached out to him and he sounds like he is getting better."

"And you are going home to see him?"

Charlotte nods.

Dr. O' Farrell sighs.

"I guess we can alphabetize them as the students hand them in and split them up before we lock up the classroom for the night. Then you are free to go on your merry way and abandon me."

"I'll get a lot of grading done on the train," Charlotte points out.

"I suppose you will." He replies loftily. "Maybe I should give you the lot."

Charlotte shrugs. "If you really want—"

"Of course I don't," he snaps in reply. "I'm not going to add to your workload when you have so much going on."

Charlotte blinks back tears, overcome with sudden emotion.

"You alright? Something in your eye?" He leans in close to inspect her and she flushes crimson. She tries to back away and trips on one of the piles of books on the floor and careens into his arms. He catches her without a thought.

And there she is, Dr. O' Farrell's arms wrapped around her, her face gazing up into his, their mouths inches apart. They stare at each other for a beat, his eyes flickering to her lips. Then he lets her go and she stumbles back, cautious of the piles all around her.

"So, so I'll see you tomorrow then?" She stammers, looking at the desk, the ground, the wall, anywhere but the professor's face. She is afraid of what she will see there.

"Yeah, yeah, of course, See you then." He mumbles and retreats behind the mountain of papers stacked atop his desk.

# CHAPTER TEN

## FORTIS MANE

The train rattles along the tracks, jostling its passengers into a restive stupor just as a mother rocks the infant in her arms to sleep. Strips of buttery sunlight stream through the windows, long black shadows stretch beneath the limbs of trees waving at the train as it speeds past.

Charlotte slumps against the window, her head thudding gently against the glass. Her eyes flicker beneath closed lids, dreams chasing away her thoughts.

A chime splits the air and a voice begins to speak. She starts awake, blinking away visions of the professor's arms around her, her mouth only inches away from his own. She remains in her seat, motionless, as her fellow passengers clamber to their feet to fight their way along the narrow aisles. Only once the car is empty she stands. Pulling her carry-on up over her shoulder she grabs her small suitcase from the overhead compartment and makes her way off the train.

The sky is a dishwater grey, the ground covered by a thin layer of quickly melting snow, and underneath it soft mud. Charlotte steps onto the grass to avoid a careless passenger and slips on the soft mud, her legs flying out beneath her. She lands with a thud and lays there a moment, trying to catch her breath. Cautiously, she rises to her feet and looks down with a groan, her hip and left leg are entirely coated with mud. She looks up and meets the disapproving stare of her mother.

"You better change before you get in my car." Is all she says.

Charlotte sighs and heads into the station to change, glad she overpacked.

The ride home is a silent one. Charlotte glances over at her mother several times, attempting to make conversation, but each time her words are met with pursed lips and hunched shoulders. Soon she gives up and sets her head against the window, and tries not to think of Dr. O' Farrell.

They arrive home. The house is dark and cold. There are no welcoming smells of onions simmering in butter, no wafts of cinnamon or pumpkin, no bright tablecloths or wreaths of fall leaves. The house is quiet as a tomb.

"Are we not making dinner this year?" Charlotte asks the retreating form of her mother. Her mother pauses a moment.

"They are having a dinner at the hospital. No sense in making a second dinner."

She walks away, leaving Charlotte alone in the doorway.

She drags her bags up the stairs, the familiar creak of the stairs the only welcome home for her. She hurries to her room, avoiding looking across the hall at the room opposite. Though she has reconciled with her brother, she has no desire to relive that awful night.

She nudges the door open and finds that her mother has used her room as a storage closet, boxes cover almost every surface, the bed, the desk, the stretch of floor by the door.

Charlotte sets her bags down with a sigh and makes a path to the bed.

Finally she gets ready for bed. She draws the covers up around her and reaches for her phone to set an alarm for the morning when a text from an unfamiliar number pops up on her screen

**Hope everything is going well on the home front!**

Charlotte stares at the text trying to decipher who it is from.

**Sorry, who is this?**

**You wound me Grey!**

A grin spreads across her face.

**Dr. O' Farrell?**

**The one and only! How are things?**

Charlotte struggles a moment, her instinct to say everything is fine but decides to be honest.

**Not the greatest. My mother isn't speaking to me. My room is now a storage closet. There are no decorations, no food. I don't even know why I came.**

His response is not immediate. He takes time to consider his words.

**You know why you had to go. You knew it wasn't going to be easy but you made the right decision. Stay strong Grey :)**

Charlotte smiles and sets the phone next to her bed, the professor's words echoing in her mind.

Charlotte spends the morning on her own, a hasty note left on the fridge letting her know that her mother is out running errands. The dinner at the hospital isn't until 5:00pm so Charlotte settles into her room with a cup of tea and does some reading for her thesis. Before she knows it, it is time to leave.

Charlotte puts on a cheery yellow cable knit sweater and floral skirt and stuffs a care package she put together for her brother in her bag. The care package includes Geoff's favourite snacks and his favourite comic book.

Her mother is waiting in the driveway, clouds of grey exhaust fumes dance in the cold. Charlotte hops into the passenger seat and braces herself for another silent drive.

The hospital isn't too far and Charlotte finds they are there sooner than she thought they would be. As her mother slams the driver's seat shut Charlotte finds she cannot move from her own seat. The thought of seeing Geoff makes her stomach plummet, makes a hand wrench at her heart. She closes her eyes and inhales. Her mother raps impatiently on the window. Charlotte exhales in a rush and exits the car.

They check in at the front desk and are given visitor's badges. An orderly escorts them to the psychiatric floor, a keycard is needed in order to enter.

Unease clenches at Charlotte's insides and her heart begins to race. She looks through the open doors of the rooms they pass, some beds are empty, some contain small groups of people visiting for the holiday, others contain only one solitary figure sitting on the bed, their gaze focused straight ahead. Charlotte whips her head away, deciding not to pry. The orderly stops at a room at the end of the hall. Her mother bustles in, her visits are routine now. She does not give any thought to Charlotte's discomfort.

Charlotte lingers at the door. The sharp, sterile smell of disinfectant stings her nose. The bright fluorescent lights flicker overhead. She inhales deeply, holds the breath, then exhales. She enters the room.

The room resembles any other hospital room, beige walls barren of decoration, standard thin sheets and blanket cover a twin bed shoved into the corner. And her brother leaps from his perch on the bed and rushes to her, her arms opening automatically as he approaches. As she wraps her arms around her brother, that fractured bond between them seems to shift. It is not mended yet, but it is on its way.

"I'm so glad you're here," Geoffrey says, giving his sister a squeeze before he withdraws from her. As he moves away Charlotte's eyes flicker down to his wrists, relieved to see there are no bandages there. Geoffrey catches her looking and bares them to her. While there are no bandages, matching silver scars cross both wrists, the sight making dread wash through her.

"It doesn't hurt. Not anymore." Geoff says quietly, looking down at his scars.

"Enough of that," their mother interrupts. "Dinner is being served in the cafeteria. Shall we go?" She slings an arm around Geoff's shoulders, draws him close for a kiss. She does not look at Charlotte as she leads Geoffrey out of the room.

Charlotte follows. She feels her phone buzz in her pocket. She reached for it and draws it out, the screen lighting up with a text.

**Stay Strong Grey.**

# CHAPTER ELEVEN

## GRATIAS

The cafeteria is as white and sterile as the hallways. Small tables are scattered throughout the room. A few patients sit there with a family member or two, but most tables are empty. The hospital staff made an attempt to liven up the place, colourful tablecloths of fall leaves are draped over the tabletops, centrepieces of fake gourds lay around the plastic cutlery. Charlotte's mother chooses one of the tables in the centre of the room and her children follow behind her. The three of them sit and wait silently for the food. One of the hospital administration enters the cafeteria with a cheerful smile plastered on her face.

"Welcome everyone! It is so wonderful to see our patients enjoy the holiday with their families. What a turn out!" Charlotte glances at the empty tables and tries not to wince. "We at Lowood Hospital would like to thank you for coming today. Now, enough chit chat! I know you all didn't come here today to hear me talk!" She pauses, expectant smile faltering a little when her joke does not land. "Happy Thanksgiving everybody!" She steps dramatically away from the door to allow the staff to wheel around their trays of food.

A young woman in a hairnet with a tired smile wheels over to their table. Charlotte murmurs her thanks to the woman and looks down at two slices of greyish turkey, a small mound of mashed potatoes, stuffing garnished with large leaves of green parsley, wilted green beans all topped off with a puddle of watery gravy. She smiles brightly across the table at her brother and shoves a mouthful of potatoes in her mouth, trying to suppress the sob that is fighting to escape her throat.

While theirs had never been the happiest of families, her mother had always made an effort over the holidays. As Charlotte gulps down her cup of cranberry juice she longs for her mother's glazed carrots, roasted Brussels sprouts and homemade bread. She misses the ritual of getting up at 6:00 am to prepare the stuffing and get the turkey in the oven in time for dinner, chopping vegetables at the table with her mother while listening to old records. The absence of that ritual feels like a searing pain in Charlotte's chest.

Geoff does not seem to mind, he chatters away about his group sessions, about what he was able to watch on the television that day, and the card game another patient has started teaching him.

"It's called Cribbage," he says in between mouthfuls of turkey, "I know it sounds like a game only old ladies play but it's fun. I'll teach you sometime."

"I'd like that." Charlotte replied.

Geoff smiles happily back at her and sets his plastic fork down. "So, how is it going at Thornfield? Getting lots of work done?"

Charlotte brightens at the chance to describe her program but as she opens her mouth to answer she is interrupted by her mother's snort of derision.

"Work? What does your sister know about real work? Here I am working full time to support this family, to support my son in the hospital, and where is she? Swanning off to some useless school to get a useless degree and for what? You think you'll ever be able to get a real job once you are finally finished? What a waste of time and money. You may as well follow them into the kitchens," she nods towards the young girl in the hairnet bringing out dessert, "that's the only job you'll be able to find once you're finished. *If* you finish that is."

"What do you mean by that?" The words tumble from her numb lips. She always knew her mother didn't approve of her choice to pursue a master's degree, but to hear her give voice to her disapproval is another thing entirely.

After an entire day of silent treatment, Charlotte's mother finally looks at her. Though a smile twists her lips, it does not reach her eyes, her eyes are as dead and cold as the night they found Geoff on the floor of his room.

"Remember your art lessons? You begged and begged to go, saved up for over a year to take that after school program. And then what? You come home in tears and never go back again. You knew then that you didn't have what it takes to be an artist, so you quit and settled on art history instead. Looking at the work of real artists and tearing it to pieces, as if you could ever paint something like that yourself. And for what? To live in la la land deluding yourself that you are talented, that you are important. Once your program is done you're back in the real world with no real skills, no real job, no real future. That is, if you do finish. My bet is you quit by Christmas." She sits back in her chair and crosses her arms, looking out at the empty tables. "Waste of time." She repeats.

Charlotte tries to respond but the words have dried up in her throat. The young woman in the hairnet comes over to their table and clears their plates and lays out their dessert of pumpkin pie, the dollop of whip cream runs in trails of milky white and pools on the plate. She is cold, her mind a distant place, where all words are foreign. She doesn't know what to say. She glances over at Geoff. Her brother is staring down at the table, his fist clenches around the plastic fork. Charlotte sees a flash of that pale hand, the discarded knife, and she pushes herself away from the table. Her mother's head whips in her direction, a look of triumph on her face. At last, she would get the fight she is waiting for, she would get to say all the bitter words she has saved up.

But Charlotte wouldn't give her the chance.

She steps over to Geoff's side of the table and envelops him in a hug which he does not return, his body is taut, bracing for the fight he fears will come. Despite her best efforts, a tear gathers in the corner of her eye and trails down her cheek, she buries her face in Geoff's shoulder, hoping that her mother doesn't see it. When she straightens the tears are gone, she puts on a smile so bright it rivals that of the hospital administrator's, and she kneels next to her brother.

"It was great to see you but I better be going, I've got a lot of exams to mark for Dr. O' Farrell. Thanks for dinner. I'm so stuffed I don't think I can finish my pie!" She grabs her plate and slides it across the table to Geoff. "You better finish it off for me." She winks at Geoff.

 

"Well, I'm not finished, if you think I'm dropping everything to drive you home—" Her mother begins hotly, another ready tirade spilling from her lips but Charlotte cuts her off.

"Of course not. I'll get a ride back."

"Couldn't be bothered to stay long could you?"

Charlotte tenses but does not rise to the bait.

"Bye, mom."

Charlotte turns her back on her family and hurries out of the cafeteria. Once she bursts out of the entrance of the hospital the tears finally flow. A sob rips free from her throat and she leans against the doorway, shoulders shuddering with the force of her sobs.

She feels a buzzing in her coat pocket and digs around for her phone. The screen lights up, illuminating her tearstained face. She can't make out the number through her tear-filled eyes. She accepts the call and presses the phone to her ear.

"Grey! How goes the familial gathering?" The familiar voice does nothing to ease her sadness, instead she is racked with sobs. The voice on the phone sharpens. "What happened? Are you alright?"

"No. No I'm not."

"Hang on, Grey. I'm coming to get you."

# CHAPTER TWELVE

## CLAIR DE LUNE

Charlotte takes a taxi to her mother's house and gathers her things together. She gazes around what was once her bedroom, now her mother's storage closet. She tears down the last of her clothes hanging in the closet, she gathers her picture frames, her sentimental knickknacks and photos and shoves them into her small suitcase. She would not be coming back.

She takes her time carrying her things down the stairs, bidding a last, silent farewell to her family home. She piles her things at the door, she begins to put on her coat and wait outside for Dr. O' Farrell to arrive, but something makes her pause.

She sets down her keys, her coat. She climbs the stairs once more and makes her way down the poorly lit hallway that featured so much in her dreams, her nightmares. She stands before the door to her brother's room and takes a breath. She eases the door open. There is no pale hand, no knife, no blood stains upon the carpet. It is just a room.

There is nothing to be afraid of anymore.

The doorbell chimes and Charlotte races down the stairs and opens the door.

Dr. Ellis O'Farrell stands on her porch, stamping his feet, his hands deep within his coat pockets, his breath escaping from his lips in wisps of white that dissipate into the night air.

"Fucking freezing out tonight!" He says in greeting.

Charlotte bursts into tears.

Dr. O' Farrell leaps forward, close enough that she can feel the cold that still clings to him. He gently ushers her inside and shuts the door.

"You alright?" He asks gently, head ducked, his brown eyes peering into her own.

She chokes back a sob and tries to pull herself together.

"I'm sorry. I'm sorry. I'm a mess. Thank you for coming," she says.

"Of course. Anything for you, Grey."

She cries harder at that, the last of her composure shattering. Her shoulders heave with sobs and she feels herself falling to the floor. But a pair of strong hands catch her and draw her close. She buries her face in the curve of his shoulder and lets the tears flow freely.

After was seems like an eternity, the tears stop. But she does not pull away from that embrace. Not right away. She leans into him, a soft sigh escaping from her lips. His hands move in soothing circles on her back. He is the one to draw away first, and Charlotte keenly feels the chill of the air between them, she mourns the absence of those hands upon her shoulders.

"Alright?" He asks gruffly, his voice low.

She looks into his face, expecting to find pity. But his face is so open, the emotion shining in his eyes frightens her.

"Yeah," she draws a hand across her face. To wipe away a tear or to hide herself from his piercing gaze?

"Is this everything?" He asks, gesturing to her suitcase by the door.

"Yeah. That's everything. Oh! You don't have to do that—" she protests as he takes her suitcase and moves to the door.

"Don't be daft, Grey."

"Really, let me, the suitcase is so old if you don't hold it a certain way the wheels won't work."

In response he lifts the suitcase off the ground entirely and winks at her over his shoulder.

"I'll meet you at the car."

The door shuts behind him.

Charlotte gazes around at the place she once called home. A place she has been so afraid of coming back to. It's just an empty house now. She eases her coat over her shoulders, lifts her bag. She steps outside into the cold, night air. She turns her key in the lock, the cold metal biting into her palm.

Then, she twists the key off of the ring and places it in the mailbox next to the door for her mother to find. The key clangs in the metal mailbox in a final farewell.

She turns her back on the house and walks over to Dr. O' Farrell.

The drive back to Thornfield is not a quiet one. While Charlotte does not have the energy to speak, Dr. O' Farrell fills the silence with his chatter. He tells her of the dinner his mother-in-law had catered to her house, how the food was delicious but the company lacking.

  MEAGAN CLEVELAND

"It's not that we don't get along, it's just, after years of just the two of us we're running out of things to say to one another. Yet we carry on the ritual of getting together for holidays, all to appease the memory of my late wife. At first it was a nice way to remember her, together, but now it feels as if we are sitting down to dinner with a ghost." He sighs and reaches forwards to fiddle with the dials of the radio. Classical music floods the car. Charlotte recognizes the first mournful notes of Debussy's *Clair de Lune*. She leans her head against the cool window and heaves a small sigh.

"Alright? Warm enough? Do you want me to turn the heat up?" He babbles, reaching for another dial.

Charlotte turns to him with a weary smile. "I'm alright."

"Good." He smiles briefly at her and then turns his head forward. They listen to the music in silence, the notes rising to a crescendo between them. It is not an uncomfortable silence, but the warm quiet between two friends enjoying their time together.

"So, as I was saying. My mother-in-law ordered way too much food for two people. She gave me all the left overs too. I don't know how I'll get through it all."  He glances over at her, then away. "I was wondering, after the disaster of a Thanksgiving you had with your family…fancy coming round to mine tomorrow? Help me get through those leftovers?"

Charlotte does not reply right away, her words are stuck in her throat. He turns his head to look at her, taking her silence as her refusal, an apology ready on his lips. But Charlotte speaks before he can.

"I'd love to," her voice breaks as she says the word love. She clears her throat. Dr. O'Farrell smiles and turns back to the road.

"Since you'll be coming over to mine tomorrow anyways, do you want me to drop you off at your apartment or do you want to stay the night? In the spare bedroom of course," he adds hastily.

Charlotte bites her lip. She knows that Adele does not approve of how close she and the professor are already, what would she say if she spent the night at his place?

But then again, what business is it of Adele's what Charlotte chooses to do?

"Sure, I'll stay the night as well." She agrees. "I don't want to be alone in my apartment tonight."

Dr.O'Farrell grimaces in sympathy, taking one hand off the steering wheel, his fingers interlacing with hers.

He holds her hand until they return to Thornfield.

# CHAPTER THIRTEEN

## DOMUM

There is nothing so excellent as a companionable silence.

The music swells between them, her hand clasped within his. Charlotte feels at ease at last. She rests her head against the window, the cold of the glass a welcome respite to the warmth in her cheeks.

The Overture to Tchaikovsky's *Romeo and Juliet* plays, the trills of the woodwinds washing over her. She glances over at Dr. O' Farrell and smiles. He does not look away from the road but squeezes her hand gently.

All too soon the ride is over, her hand bereft of his touch, as he places both hands on the wheel to turn into the driveway. The driveway is framed by the gently swaying boughs of maple and birch trees. A five bay, Georgian Style house peeks out from behind two tall pines which stand sentinel before it.

She eases out of the car while he gathers her suitcase from the trunk. As he moves around the car to join her, she takes in the sight of his home.

The house is square, with rows of symmetrical windows, twin chimneys and covered in cheerful red bricks which stand in stark comparison to the austere slate grey of the shutters.

As they make their way up to the door, Charlotte half expects to see a historical plaque affixed it.

"What are you looking at?" Dr. O' Farrell asks as he digs in his pockets for his keys.

"Your house. It looks like the house from a period drama." She jokes.

"It's pretty old." He replies simply, turning his key in the lock. The door opens with a groan and Dr. O' Farrell shoulders his way inside.

Charlotte expects the interior of the house to be a bigger version of his office, with austere mahogany surfaces littered with books and loose sheaves of paper. She expects the inside of the house to be dim, the light of day hidden behind dusty curtains, the only light coming from a roaring fireplace. She expects wingback armchairs, globes, possibly a telescope to view the stars.

She does not expect what lays within.

Everything is bright and airy. For such a square, squat house, she did not expect the high ceilings, the crown molding, the walls bisected with white wainscoting and light blue damask wallpaper. An ornate credenza sits prettily by the door, and Charlotte does not see any wingback chairs, but chaise lounges of luxe velvet, dainty ribbon back chairs and large gilded mirrors. Dr. O' Farrell wheels her suitcase over to the stairs and Charlotte drifts into what must be the drawing room, decorated in the same blue damask. There is a fireplace, but no fire, the inside of the fireplace is stacked with books that were put in spine first so that only their white pages are visible. Everything is neat and orderly. Everything is so not Dr. O' Farrell.

She hears his footsteps behind her, and says without turning around, "I'm surprised by your interior decorating choices. This is not at all how I pictured the inside of your house."

He does not reply right away. His silence unnerving her, she turns round to face him. His eyes are averted, taking in the room and trying to see it through her eyes. He rubs a hand down his face.

"It wouldn't look like me would it? Antoinette picked everything out. This is all her." Silence stretches out painfully between them and Charlotte feels the ghost of the other woman appraising her.

"I didn't have the heart to change anything after she died." He looks around mournfully.

"It's very beautiful." Charlotte offers.

"Yeah." He spins on his heel and faces her at last, a weary smile brightening his face.

"Shall I show you your room?"

Charlotte nods and Dr. O' Farrell takes hold of her suitcase and hauls it up the stairs.

Charlotte trails behind him, taking her time as she makes her way up the stairs to gaze in disbelief at the tinkling crystal chandelier that swings gently from the crown moulding that adorns the high ceiling.

The professor's house makes her think of fairytales. While she expected the dilapidated, crumbling manor of the beast, she finds herself in the palatial home fitting of a princess. The house itself feels like the enchanted castle from Sleeping Beauty, a sleeping enchantment cast over the building, waiting for its mistress to awaken.

But she never would. She is gone from this world and the house, however beautifully decorated it seemed, is cold. A home for ghosts.

Charlotte pauses as she passes over the last step. At the top of the staircase hangs a large frame, depicting a wedding photo. Dr. O' Farrell looks the same, but lighter somehow, his face devoid of that heavy sadness forever tugging at the corner of his lips. His head is thrown back in laughter, a beautiful woman clutching at his arm and smiling widely at him. She is tall and slim, with masses of blonde hair cascading down her back. She is the living picture of Botticelli's *Venus,* a goddess come to earth.

She leans forward to get a better look, her fingertips brushing across the gilded frame. The picture frame swings forward dangerously and Charlotte reaches out to grab it before it crashes to the floor. The frame smacks her in the face and Charlotte bites the inside of her lip so hard she tastes blood. After the panic of the moment passes she carefully places the frame back onto the wall and turns away to follow Dr. O' Farrell. The portrait hangs crookedly, the eyes of Antoinette O'Farrell seem to follow her as she goes.

# CHAPTER FOURTEEN

## CARPE NOCTEM

Charlotte moves down the hallway, through stripes of light cast by the sconces mounted on the wall. Dr. O'Ellis stands beside the door but does not enter. He waits for her to join him, for her to reach her hand forward and push the door open.

The walls are covered in wood panelling painted a calming sage green, an ebony four poster bed sits in the centre of the room, a toile bedspread is draped over top. A bookshelf is built into the very walls themselves, the shelves full of the classics: Austen, Bronte, Carroll and Dickens. The room looks like something out of a period drama, and Charlotte feels like she is encroaching on the true heroine's space.

"Did Antoinette decorate this room too?" She asks.

"She decorated the whole house." Dr. O' Farrell replies. He strides over to the bookshelf and pulls out a copy of Daphne du Maurier's *Rebecca* and leafs idly through its pages before returning it to the shelves. He looks up and meets her eyes for a single, breathless moment, then looks away. "I chose the books though."

"Fan of the classics huh?" Charlotte smiles.

"Oh yeah," He grins. "I used to watch the films with my Gran. They remind me of her." He looks around the room. "This is the only room in the entire house that isn't blue. Green was Gran's favourite colour. Antoinette and I had a huge row over it actually. But Gran was coming to stay and I wanted this room ready for her."

"So you *did* have a hand in decorating. This room at least."

He purses his lips a moment. "Yeah. One room in the whole house." He meets her eyes again but does not look away. "It's yours. For now."

"What about your Gran?"

His eyes shutter a moment. "She doesn't need it anymore."

"I'm sorry." Charlotte covers his hand with her own.

Dr. O' Farrell shrugs. "It's alright. It was years ago now. This house has had it's fair share of death." He interlaces his fingers with hers. "I think it's time to liven the place up again."

He smiles at her and Charlotte feels heat in her cheeks. He glances at her rosy cheeks and steps away.

"Well, it's getting late. I'll let you head to bed and I'll see you in the morning?"

She nods, not trusting herself to speak.

"Goodnight." He says, stepping towards her a moment, his body so close to hers she feels the heat rising from his skin. "Goodnight my—" he starts to say then seems to swallow the words. She leans towards him and he steps back. He leaves without another word, shutting the door behind him.

"Goodnight." She replies to the closed door.

She turns away and does not see the shadow that remains on the other side of her door.

 MEAGAN CLEVELAND

Charlotte wheels her suitcase over to the wardrobe in the corner. She opens the doors and finds the inside empty so begins to fill it with the clothes she packed for the weekend.

She changes into her pyjamas and pulls back the bedspread and crawls underneath, suddenly exhausted.

She closes her eyes and tries to forget the bite of her mother's words, the sadness in her brother's eyes. Instead she thinks of *Clair de Lune* and a warm hand clasped around her own.

Charlotte starts awake. Something has woken her, but she doesn't know what. She rises from the bed and crosses carefully across the rug to the door. The hallway is cloaked in shadow, the darkness seemingly muffling all sound. But— there. She hears something. A rush of noise.

The sharp scent of smoke stings her nostrils and an orange glow shines from the door to Dr. O' Farrell's room.

Without thinking, Charlotte races down the hall and shoulders her way into the professor's bedroom.

Dr. O' Farrell's room is engulfed in flames.

"Dr. O' Farrell wake up! Wake up!" She screams, rushing towards the bed and stopping short at the flames that dance across the space between them.

"Dr. O' Farrell! Dr. O' Farrell!" She screams again and again.

And then.

"Ellis! Wake up!"

And from his place on the bed, his eyes flutter open.

"Grey?" He begins to rise from the bed then notices the flames. "Fuck! Are you trying to kill me again? I thought we were past that?"

"How can you joke at a time like this!" She cries out, exasperated. She looks frantically around the room and spots a large vase full of bright sunflowers. She races over, grabs the flowers and throws them to the ground, grasping the vase in both hands she turns back towards the bed and dumps its contents over the fire. The flames go out with a hiss, and dark plumes of smoke waft up around her. She starts to cough and almost drops the vase, but a pair of strong, sure, hands take it from her and set it aside. Dr. O' Farrell has crossed the space between them, the scorched coverlet of his bed forgotten, his eyes are fixed on her.

"You alright?"

"Me?" She replies in-between bouts of coughing. "You're the one who almost burned to a crisp in your own bed! What happened?"

"Oh." He looks away, sheepish for a moment. "Smoking in bed."

She gapes at him.

"Smoking? In bed?" She glances at the pack of cigarettes on the bedside table. "Are you crazy?"

He raises his hands in defence. "I almost died. You should be nicer to me."

"Nicer? I saved your life. Again!"

"Is that what you call it? Seems like an awful coincidence that I keep getting into these situations you need to save me from, Grey."

Her grins at her and looks down at her quivering hands.

"You alright?"

"I was so scared."

He steps closer, taking her hands in his.

"Of the fire?"

She shakes her head.

"That you might get hurt." She whispers.

He inhales sharply. Closes his eyes and grimaces, as if in pain. Then pulls her towards him, his arms wrapping around her, holding her so close to him that she can feel his heart racing. She buries her face in his chest. He gasps but doesn't pull away, instead his arms grip her tighter.

"I'm sorry I scared you." He says softly. She likes the way she can feel the words rumble in his chest. He pulls away from her so that he can peer down into her face. "Thanks for saving me Grey." He smiles at her and she can't help but smile back.

He looks past her a moment and she follows his gaze to the sunflowers scattered across the floor. To the blackened covers that lay in a heap on the floor.

"I'm sorry I made a mess." She apologizes.

Dr. O' Farrell shrugs. "Not to worry Grey, I'll clean it up in the morning."

"But where will you sleep?"

The words seem to hang in the air between them and Charlotte wishes desperately that she can take them back.

"The couch'll be grand. Not to worry Grey." He winks at her, then slings an arm around her shoulders and steers her to the door, down the hall and to her room. He stops outside her door.

"You've had a rough day. You need to rest."

"I had a rough day?" She replies nodding in the direction of his room. He barks out a laugh.

"We've both had a rough day. But things will be better in the morning. Goodnight, Grey."

"Goodnight, Dr. O' Farrell."

He doesn't move away. Not yet.

"You don't have to call me that you know." He says quietly.

"What should I call you then?"

"What name did you use to wake me up?"

There is a beat of silence between them.

"If I start calling you by your name, you need to start calling me by mine." She retorts.

"Alright." He steps towards her and presses his lips to her forehead.

"Goodnight, Charlotte."

"Goodnight, Ellis."

# CHAPTER FIFTEEN

## IN MEMORIAM

The hallway is empty, Dr. O' Farrell's room is deserted, the scorched and sodden bedclothes gone, the vase sits upright, the sunflowers stand tall within it.

It was as if last night never happened.

But.

If you raise your eyes up you can see the dark stain that reaches down from the ceiling, the acrid smell of smoke lingers. The entire house is freezing cold, the gauzy white curtains billowing outwards. The windows are open, airing out the smell of the fire.

Last night really did happen.

Charlotte presses her fingers to her forehead, her fingertips searching for the memory of his lips.

She walks back down the hall to her room to get dressed.

She pulls out one of her old dresses she grabbed from her closet at home, a grey sweater dress she is grateful for now that the chill of the winter air has crept into the house. She pulls on a pair of leggings and a thick pair of socks and faces herself in the mirror. How strange that so much has changed in just one day, yet she looks the same.

She scrapes her hair back into a sleek bun and makes her way downstairs.

She knows Dr. O' Farrell is in the kitchen from the great deal of noise he is making. She stands in the hallway, not daring to encroach into his space, not yet. Instead she observes him.

He is standing at the oven, a white apron tied around his waist, his back to her. He takes a step back and flicks his wrist and a pancake flutters into the air and back into the pan. Whistling he sets the pan back onto the burner and waits. When it is time he slides the pancake onto a plate and begins again.

Charlotte smiles as she watches him, leaning against the door to the kitchen. The hinges squeal in protest against her weight and Dr. O' Farrell spins around.

"Good morning."

"Good morning." Charlotte murmurs, padding over to stand next to him and peer over his shoulder.

"Hope you like pancakes." He thrusts a plate at her and steers her over to the kitchen table. "Eat."

She takes her place at one end of the table and he takes his place at the other. They eat in silence. When the pancakes are gone Dr. O' Farrell leaps to his feet and whisks the plates away.

"I can clear up," Charlotte offers, rising from her chair.

Dr. O'Farrell puts his hands on her shoulders and gently presses her back into her seat.

"You're a guest. Sit."

She obeys and watches him, bemused, as he clangs and crashes around the kitchen. When the kitchen is clean at last he turns to face her.

"So. What shall we do today? All we need to do for dinner is to heat up the leftovers so we've most of the day free. What's it to be?"

Charlotte glances out the window. Though there is a chill to the air, the day is bright and the sun is shining.

"We could go for a walk?"

"Sure."

The sky is a brilliant blue, the clouds like gossamer threads, and though the trees are stripped bare of their leaves their naked branches seem to wave as Charlotte and Dr. O' Farrell amble past.

"What is a typical Thanksgiving like for you?" She asks.

"Well, I never had Thanksgiving until I moved here to teach. I was new to the country, new to teaching, and very much alone here. Until I met Antoinette. She knew I had nowhere to go for the holiday weekend so she invited me round to hers, to spend the weekend with her and her mother. Antoinette's mother is rather a grand lady and she isn't one for cooking herself so she had the meal catered and we spent the day listening to old records and looking at old photographs."

"Sounds nice."

"It was a bit weird for me at first, having all those photo albums thrust at me, and being shown photo after photo of people I don't know. Listening to songs that had no meaning to me, having all their shared stories explained to me. I always felt a bit like an intruder. Then, after Antoinette died, we held on to that tradition, but now all the photos are photos of *her*, the songs are songs we played at our wedding. It became a day to remember her."

"Do you miss her?"

He stops and Charlotte stops beside him. He squints into the morning sunshine, looking away from her.

"Of course I do. But not like before. Before it was a desperate thing, clinging to every little thing that reminded me of her, no matter how painful it was. Now it feels like I have buried myself in memories of her, and the more I remember the less meaningful the memories become."

He sighs, and looks at her at last. A frown tugs at the corners of his lips and Charlotte longs to reach out and touch him, to make him smile again.

A cloud passes overhead and a shadow falls over them. Dr. O' Farrell's face is pale and worn, his eyes ringed with dark circles.

"You tend to remember the good at first. But as the years go on the bad memories start to take over. Our marriage wasn't on the best of terms when we found out she was sick. But what could I do, how could I possibly leave when she needed me the most? It's hard to watch someone waste away like that, to watch someone so bright and full of life fade. She said some things I rather wish I could forget, near the end. And I said some things I wish I could take back."

Charlotte frowns, thinking of the beautiful woman in the photograph, her eyes fixed on her husband, her hand grasping at his arm possessively.

"So why keep up the tradition? Why stay in that house that is all hers, why torture yourself with memories that only hurt you?" Charlotte blurts out.

"Because I deserve it." He snaps.

Charlotte draws back at the tone and his face softens.

 

"Sorry. Sorry, I didn't mean to snap. I don't really want to talk about it anymore, okay?"

Charlotte nodes and they start walking again.

The clouds pass and the sun shines again, the trees tremble in the breeze as they pass.

# CHAPTER SIXTEEN

## FESTUM

It is past midnight on Thanksgiving day, empty plates and dishes litter every available surface in the kitchen. Though dinner ended some hours before they remain in their seats, leaning towards each other from opposite sides of the table with only candlelight and stories between them.

They have spoken of their childhoods, their adulthoods so far, and have now moved on to education. Dr. O' Farrell is regaling Charlotte with stories of how he had attended an all boys, Catholic high school run by priests.

"I expect you were a little devil at school?" Charlotte smiles, imagining him as a young boy. Dr. O' Farrell shakes his head.

"Not at all! I was good as gold, a choir boy and everything."

"You sing?"

"Used to. Maybe one day you'll get to hear me." He winks. Charlotte laughs and takes a long sip from her wine glass.

"And you?"

Charlotte swallows and sets down her glass. "Same. Good grades, clubs, choir, girl guides—"

"Girl guides?" He interrupts, his eyes wide. "You mean with the sashes and the badges and the selling biscuits?"

"Cookies," She corrects then nods. "Yep. I was the good girl. It was Geoff who was the little devil, he was always getting into trouble at school, always being sent to the principal's office. But it was never a punishment, the office administration *loved* him. They always felt so sorry for poor little Geoffrey, acting out to get his mother's attention. Not that she ever paid any attention. Not to me and my grades, or Geoff and his detentions."

Silence hangs heavy in the air and Charlotte seems to break from the spell and looks around, taking in the darkness outside, the dishes everywhere. "It's so late. Why don't I start clearing up?" She stands, the legs of her chair squealing in protest at the movement. Dr. O' Farrell rises as well.

"No no, let me, you're the guest remember," he chides, leaning over to grab a serving platter, the same platter that Charlotte was reaching for. Their fingers brush against each other and Charlotte feels the contact like a static shock. She jumps a little and draws back. He pauses, then grabs the platter and turns around, carrying it over to the sink. Charlotte shakes her head and collects as many plates as she can, piling them one on top of the other, and bears her stack over to the sink which is now filling with warm water, a froth of bubbles threatening to tumble over onto the counter. His back is to her, but as she approaches he extends a wet hand. Charlotte places a plate into his grasp and he begins to wash. Soon the table is clear, the dishes drying on the rack next to the sink.

"Fancy a cup of tea?"

Charlotte looks around at the darkened windows. "Isn't a bit late for tea?"

"Never." Dr. O' Farrell fills the kettle and sets it on the stove to boil. They stand in the kitchen and wait.

"Well, what now?"

"Would you like to show me some pictures? Play me some songs? Like your tradition with you mother-in-law?"

Dr. O' Farrell does not answer He stares at her until the kettle begins to whistle. He turns his back to her to take it off the element. He pours the water into a teapot and tosses two teabags inside. Then he turns back to her, his face tired, a frown tugging at his lips.

"No. Anything but that. I'd like to make some new traditions."

Charlotte stares at him a moment then walks out of the kitchen, up the stairs and into her bedroom. She kneels next to her suitcase to rifle through its contents. She hears the floorboards creak behind her and knows that Dr. O' Farrell has followed her. But she does not turn around. Not yet. She is still looking.

She digs through rolled up pairs of socks, and scarves wadded into balls until she finds it. When she had yanked her old clothes from her closet at home and tossed them into her suitcase she also tossed in some of the other contents of her closet, including an old edition of Trivial Pursuit. She holds it aloft in triumph, and turns around with a grin.

"A board game? Really?"

"Come on, it will be fun!"

And it is. Charlotte sets up while Dr. O' Farrell pours out the tea and they play until the pot is empty. Charlotte's circle is full of all the different colour wedges needed to win, Dr. O' Farrell has half as many and a scowl on his face.

"How do you even know all this? All these events are from before you were born. Some before *I* was born."

"Oh, this belonged to my grandparents. I used to play it with them so many times I learned all the answers that way."

"Cheater."

After Charlotte's second win Dr. O' Farrell pointedly folds the board and places it back into the box along with the cards and playing pieces then disappears into the kitchen. He returns with two plates.

"No, I can't possibly eat any more!" Charlotte protests, holding her hands up in defeat.

Dr. O' Farrell settles beside her on the nest of pillows and blankets they made on the floor when they played their board game.

"What is Thanksgiving for, if not to eat until you're sick? Now. Apple or pumpkin?"

In the end they cannot decide, using their forks to have one mouthful of apple pie, then a mouthful of pumpkin and cream. When only crumbs remain they set down their forks and lay back on the cushions.

Charlotte eases her head back and faces the clock.

"Is that the time? I didn't know it's so late. I better get ready for bed, I have some readings to do before classes start again." Reluctantly she rises to her feet, her battered box of Trivial Pursuit clutched to her chest.

"Thank you for the lovely day," she says.

Dr. O' Farrell remains seated, staring up at her.

"Thank you. It would have been a miserable day without you."

A laugh slips out of Charlotte's lips, thinking it another one of his jokes. The laughter dies as she realizes he is serious.

After what seems like an eternity Dr. O' Farrell rises to his feet so that he stands directly in front of Charlotte, their toes almost touching.

"Goodnight, then." He says, his voice hoarse.

"Goodnight....Ellis."

A smile lights up his face. He leans in and brushed his lips across her forehead.

"Goodnight, Charlotte."

Charlotte goes to bed with a smile on her face.

She wakes up in total darkness.

The cold winter air chills the room and Charlotte draws the covers up around her shoulders. She is unused to the heavy silence that blankets the house. As her apartment is in the downtown area, she is accustomed the sounds of the city lulling her to sleep. The sound of car horns honking, crowds murmuring on the sidewalk, the TV next-door blaring as familiar to her as any lullaby now. Dr. O' Farrell's house is on the outskirts of the city, practically in the country.

Charlotte expects the country to be quiet. And it is. But because it is so quiet she hears things that never bothered her before. The sound of the wind rushing through the trees, the branches scratching against her window like grasping hands eager to get in. The distant bark of a dog. A car door slamming shut. And that is only what is happening outside. Inside is just as loud. She never knew that old houses creak and moan in the night like a child having a bad dream. Just as her eyelids begin to flutter closed, just as her head eases back into her

          **MEAGAN CLEVELAND**

pillows, she feels it. A presence in the room. Charlotte longs to roll onto her side, to open her eyes and prove that nothing is there, that nothing is wrong. But she is frozen in place. She convinces herself that the she can't hear anything beyond the frantic beats of her heart, the rapid intake of her breath. But beyond the sounds of her own body, she swears she can hear the whine of the door hinges, the rasp of feet sliding across the wooden floorboards. She holds her breath, willing her heart to still so she can just listen, so she can hear whether someone is in the room with her.

Charlotte cannot move, she cannot breathe, she can do nothing but lay there, frozen, her eyes wide in the darkness. She lets her eyes adjust and stares at the wall. A car passes outside, and light flashes across the room and Charlotte swears she sees the shadow of a figure just behind her. The light gives her courage. Charlotte tenses then springs up and whips around, hoping that the headlights of the car will reveal the intruder. The car passes and darkness falls.

She is very much alone.

Charlottes huffs a laugh of relief, raising a shaking hand to her brow to push her hair out of her eyes. She lays back down and gathers the blankets around her. Letting the sound of the rushing wind ease her to sleep.

Her breaths are deep and even now, her heartbeat a steady staccato. But, just above the whisper of her own soft sighs, she can hear her door gently easing closed.

# CHAPTER SEVENTEEN

## TERMINUS

It is difficult for Charlotte to return to her everyday life after spending the weekend with Dr. O' Farrell. She treasures those short days of warmth and intimacy. Her lips remember the shape of the name Ellis, and she longs to say the name aloud again. But she does not have the courage to do so, now they are back on campus.

It is cold. The kind of cold that seems to freeze time itself. The clouds hang heavy above the turrets of Thornfield, so laden with snow that they seem like if you reach out and touch them they might burst. Canopies of bare branches reach for the clouds like pale hands. The campus is covered in a thick blanket of snow. Fat snowflakes fall in lazy spirals to kiss the field of white below, glittering under the weak sunlight like facets on a diamond.

It seems so peaceful.

But Charlotte does not feel at peace.

It is too cold. The damp cold of southern Ontario, cold that seeps into your bones, cold that makes each inhalation of breath feel like swallowing shards of glass. The steady snowfall muffles all sound. All she can hear is her own soft inhalations of breath, the whisper of her pen against paper.

Charlotte and Dr. O' Farrell eased back into their regular routine, the memory of their weekend spent together never spoken aloud, but shared between them.

She is sitting in Dr. O' Farrell's office. She should be grading the stack of papers on her lap but instead she stares at the snowflakes dancing upon the window. Winter has claimed Thornfield and the end of the semester is quickly approaching, as is the end of her teaching assistantship with Dr. O' Farrell.

And Charlotte is terrified.

She has spent so much time in his company that Charlotte has begun to feel as if they are one person, not two. She can no longer tell where he begins and she ends. They share one mind, one heart. And if she is forced to leave him she will be leaving half of herself behind as well.

Blinded by her own misery, she does not see Dr. O' Farrell rise from his chair and move around his desk to stand beside her. She starts when a warm hand rests on her shoulder. She looks up into the concerned face of Dr. O' Farrell.

"Charlotte?"

He speaks her name softy, like a secret, crouching down beside where she sits in her chair so their eyes are level.

"Everything okay?"

She nods.

"I'm fine."

His eyes narrow.

"You're lying."

She flinches. Bites her lips. Looks past him to the snowflakes whirling against the grey sky.

"Charlotte."

He speaks her name sharply now, his hands on her shoulders, forcing her to look at him.

"What is it?"

"The semester is almost over."

The words are barely above a whisper, as if she speaks them too loudly time will hasten and their time together will truly end.

"Yes." He responds, his brow furrowed. "What of it?"

"Our class is almost over."

He does not reply, but looks at her expectantly.

"What will happen when it ends? Will this end too?" She gestures between them.

Dr. O' Farrell inhales sharply and drops his head, their foreheads now touching. She leans into the touch, his breath is warm on her face.

"Never."

He responds, pressing closer to her, his cheek against hers, his arms enveloping her. He holds her to his chest and she can feel the steady beat of his heart against her own.

Footsteps echo in the hallway and he stiffens until the sound recedes. He eases away reluctantly.

"Don't look at it as a bad thing. Once the semester is over, your contract with me is over too. You won't be working for me anymore."

"That's what I'm afraid of." She says softly.

"Charlotte," he says, his voice pleading, begging her to understand. "You won't be working for me anymore once the semester ends. Then this," he gestures between them with a smile. "Won't be considered so inappropriate."

Her heart quickens.

"What do you mean?"

He bites his lip, his hand gripping the back of his neck. He looks away.

"You know what I mean."

"Do you mean, that after the semester is over, that we can be together?" The words tumble from her lips.

He looks at her then, his eyes burning with intensity.

He nods.

Charlotte leaves his office with a smile. She feels light, as if a great burden has been lifted from her shoulders. She walks down the hallway to her own office and she isn't surprised to find Adele at her desk. She is surprised by the stranger siting at her own desk, her chair facing Adele's, the two women mirroring each other so that each seems to be a reflection. They look so much alike. The stranger has the same blonde hair, the same large doe like eyes. But whereas Adele's face is often creased with a smile, this woman's face is artfully blank. She glances over at Charlotte and immediately looks away, dismissing her.

"Hey!" Adele says in greeting, rising from her chair. "Hey. Charlotte, look who's here! My sister came to visit."

The woman sighs and looks over at Charlotte once more. She does not stand up to greet her, yet even sitting she seems to look down on Charlotte.

"Bee, this is Charlotte. Charlotte, this is my sister Bee."

The woman rises to her feet. She looks over at Adele with a frown.

"Only my friends and family call me Bee. You can call me Blanche."

# CHAPTER EIGHTEEN

## PRANDIUM

Blanche moves through the conference room like she belongs there. All around her faces brighten with recognition, hands reach out to grasp hers, heads lean conspiratorially towards her own. She commands the room.

Charlotte on the other hand, hovers on the outskirts of the room. She clings to the corners like a forgotten cobweb, just out of reach. She has been at Thornfield for months now and has just started to feel like she has made a home here. But now she is reminded just how out of place she still is.

A large circle gathers around Blanche now, obscuring her from view. Charlotte lingers at the table laden with trays of pastries and sliced fruit, tea and coffee. She pours some tea into a paper cup but does not drink. She keeps the cup tightly grasped in her hands, the heat of the liquid it contains scalding her palms.

There is a flicker of movement at the door.

Dr. O' Farrell has arrived.

He makes a beeline to the table, grabs a flimsy paper plate and piles it high with flaky croissants, danishes drizzled with icing, and thick slices of banana bread. He balances the plate precariously on one arm and with the other reaches for the tea. Charlotte leaves her place in the corner to appear at his side with a cup.

"Thanks." He flashes her a crooked grin and her heart flutters in her chest.

While he pours she reaches for three sachets of sugar, tears their corners and pours their contents into the cup.

"Am I so predictable?' He laughs. Charlotte smiles back and brings her own cup to her lips.

The crowd parts and a voice calls out.

"Ellis, is that you?"

Blanche appears before her, nudging her out of the way so she can wrap an arm around the professor's shoulders. She leans in and presses a kiss on each of his cheeks.

Charlotte looks on, heart plummeting in her chest.

Dr. O' Farrell blinks dazedly at the woman standing before him. She has completely displaced Charlotte now. The crowd surges around them and Charlotte finds herself pushed out to the corner once again.

This time she is not alone.

Joanna has also taken root at the outskirts of the room. Her cloud of curls pulled back with colourful scarf. Her face twisted in a scowl.

"Just what I need." She mutters under her breath.

"Do you know her?"

"Dr. Blanche Sheridan. She was a grad student here when I started as an undergrad. Now she's an Associate Professor at another university. I was just starting to think we were finally rid of her." Joanna says darkly, tearing the croissant in her hand into smaller and smaller pieces, her eyes never leaving the crowd of academics currently freezing her out.

"Do you not like her?"

Joanna snorts. "That's a mild way of putting it."

The crowd parts for a moment and Charlotte sees Blanche laugh and place a hand on Dr. O' Farrell's arm.

"Everyone acts like she is some ground-breaking scholar, but there's nothing special about her research. Not to mention, she's unhinged."

Charlotte turns away from the professor to look at Joanna. "What do you mean?"

"There is something wrong with her." Joanna lowers her voice, leaning so close that Charlotte can smell her floral perfume. "When I was an undergrad they were in a relationship." She nods in the direction of Blanche and the professor. Charlotte glances over at them to see Blanche's hand is still grasping Dr. O' Farrell's arm.

"Adele told me they used to date." Charlotte murmurs.

"They did, for a few months. Dr. O' Farrell got into a lot of trouble over it with the department, so he ended things. But it wasn't over for *her*. She was always waiting outside his office, auditing his classes. Eventually she clued in that Dr. O' Farrell wasn't interested. Even after she finished her PhD and went on to teach at another university, she keeps finding an excuse to come back here. And every time she does, she zeroes in on *him*. She can't get over that he rejected her."

They turn and watch the crowd.

"But why does that matter to you?" Charlotte asks, wondering why Joanna cares so much.

"I used to be his teaching assistant, remember? We held a big conference, and Dr. Sheridan was here for a whole week, never leaving Dr. O' Farrell's side the entire time. It drove him crazy. And when he is in a bad mood, *everyone* is in a bad mood. Surely you know by now? He's awful."

Charlotte blinks in surprise.

"He isn't awful to me."

Joanna tears her gaze away from the crowd and frowns at Charlotte.

"You be careful. He has a thing for grad students, you know."

Charlotte stiffens.

"Did you...did he..." she stutters, ice spreading through her veins. Blanche was bad enough, but if Charlotte finds out there was something going on with Joanna—

"Hell no." Joanna retorts. "First of all it's completely unprofessional for him to start a relationship with a student. There's the imbalance of power, the age difference—why are you so interested?" She asks sharply. She leans closer and narrows her eyes. "Has he been inappropriate with you?" She asks quietly, her hand hovering over Charlotte's shoulder, as if she wants to comfort her but isn't sure how.

Charlotte shakes her head.

"Of course not, he's been such a good friend to me."

Joanna's eyes narrow even further.

"A friend? Charlotte, that man isn't your friend. I'm glad to hear he hasn't tried to start anything with you. But please, be careful around him."

Charlotte leaves the faculty luncheon, retreating to her office.

Her footsteps echo throughout the empty hallway, but all Charlotte hears are Joanna's words again and again.

*They were in a relationship.*

She all but runs down the hall, slamming the door shut behind her. She gasps in a breath and collapses into her chair, her head in her hands.

How could she compare to Blanche? She is the successful academic that Charlotte longs to be. She should be at the luncheon, commanding the room with her fascinating research, her witty responses. But where is she now? Hiding in her little office, on the brink of tears. What does it matter if she cries, here in her own space. Here there is no one to see, no one to judge.

Charlotte lets the tears flow, pressing her hand to her mouth to smother the sobs that threaten to escape.

She closes her eyes and sees Blanche's dainty hand on Dr. O' Farrell's arm, her fingers grasping at his sleeves. She sees the stunned look on his face as Blanche draws him in for a kiss on the cheek.

Charlotte flinches.

The door opens.

"I couldn't find you in there and—what's wrong?"

Dr. O' Farrell kneels beside her.

"Charlotte, tell me."

Charlotte shudders and turns away.

Dr. O' Farrell grips the arms of her desk chair and spins her towards him.

She turns her head away.

He sighs.

"Fine. Don't tell me. But come on back to the library with

me, they're bringing out sandwiches and I know you didn't eat a thing before. It'll make you feel better."

He smiles encouragingly at her.

She can't help but smile back.

She wipes the tears from her face and stands.

He takes her hand in his and leads her out of the office.

Back in the library Charlotte grabs a cup of lukewarm tea and knocks it back.

The table is now covered with trays of tea sandwiches: egg salad, ham and cheese, cucumber, all cut in dainty triangles, the crusts of the bread cut off.

She reaches for the tray of cucumber sandwiches, seizes one and puts it on a plate.

Dr. O' Farrell frowns at the solitary sandwich and grabs one of each, piling them on top of one another.

"Eat."

He grabs her elbow and steers her over to the widow. She picks up a sandwich and nibbles wanly at it.

Dr. O' Farrell leaves her side to grab his own plate.

While he is gone, a figure drifts over.

"Charlotte!"

Dr. Fairfax, her hair in a copper beehive, a pair of rhinestone encrusted cat's eye glasses perched on her nose, joins her at the window.

"Enjoying the food? They really put on a spread today, what with Dr. Sheridan visiting for her talk this afternoon. You'll be coming I'm sure?"

Charlotte did not plan on attending but she nods anyway. If her supervisor wants her there, she would be there.

"Anyway, that's not why I'm here. I just wanted to tell you I finished the chapters you sent me. Really good work! Your thesis is coming together nicely!"

Charlotte brightens at the mention of her research. She discusses her plans for her next chapter, not noticing the audience gathering behind her.

She is just describing the psychoanalytic theory she plans to apply to her reading of a specific painting when a snort interrupts her.

She turns to find Blanche looming over her.

Her shoulders tense in anticipation.

"Psychoanalytic theory? What happened to art for art's sake? You can't prescribe meanings to art, you don't know what the painter was thinking when they painted the piece." Blanche argues.

Charlotte can feel colour rising in her cheeks.

"I admit I can't know what the artist himself was feeling when he painted, but I can explain the feelings the painting evokes in the viewers."

Blanche lets out another snort of derision.

"You know, our modern concepts of psychoanalysis weren't even in existence at the time the artist was alive. I think its irresponsible to approach it that way—"

"Well, I think it's brilliant." A familiar voice interrupts.

Charlotte's body turns to him, like the flower turns to the sun.

"Anyway, what does it matter what we think? Art is subjective. And by contributing a new view Charlotte is engaging in scholarship. I think it's marvellous." He smiles down at her and Charlotte feels the tension leave her shoulders.

She turns to find Blanche watching her through narrowed eyes, her gaze fixed on the arm Dr. O' Farrell has slung around Charlotte's shoulders.

"I didn't realize you knew each other." Blanche says icily.

Oblivious to the tension, Dr. Fairfax cheerily interjects. "Oh yes! Charlotte is Ellis' teaching assistant this term. She's doing a marvellous job from what I've heard."

"Splendid! She tried to have me killed when we first met." Dr. O' Farrell says.

"What?" Blanche looks from Dr. O' Farrell to Dr. Fairfax, ignoring Charlotte completely.

"Oh, do you mean your accident at the start of term? I had no idea Charlotte was there."

"She was walking in the road and I swerved around her and ended up in the ditch."

"I wasn't in the middle of the road, you were speeding and the road was wet."

"I *was* speeding." He agrees. "And I would have bled to death if Charlotte hadn't called the ambulance and climbed into the ditch and got me out of the car."

"Oh Charlotte, how brave of you!" Dr. Fairfax gasps.

"Anyone would have done it." Charlotte protests.

Dr. Fairfax leans forward and places a hand on Charlotte's arm.

"Not anyone. I don't know if you know this, but Ellis here can be quite, ah, unfriendly when the mood takes him."

"Steady on, Cat." Dr. O' Farrell laughs.

　　　　MEAGAN CLEVELAND

"You can be quite the bully, you know."

"Maybe I was. But Charlotte didn't let me bully her, if anything she bullied me into submission until the ambulance arrived."

"Did you really? I should have liked to see that!" Dr. Fairfax laughs.

"You wouldn't think to look at her." Blanche mutters under her breath. Charlotte stiffens but she thinks she is the only one to have heard.

They finish their sandwiches and drinks and make their way to the lecture hall to hear Blanche's talk.

Dr. O' Farrell takes a chair beside Charlotte. As everyone settles in their seats, Dr. O' Farrell leans over.

"She's wrong, you know."

Charlotte turns to look at him. His face so close to her own that she can feel his breath on her cheek.

"You're stronger than you look, Grey."

The hall goes silent as Blanche steps up to the podium. The lights dim and darken, a projection shines on the screen.

And under the desk, Dr. O' Farrell's hand finds hers, his fingers interlacing with her own.

# CHAPTER NINETEEN

## INJURIA

Exams are just about finished and most of the undergrads, faculty and administration have gone home for the holidays. Only a few scatter-brained academics who lost track of time, exam admin counting down the minutes until they can clock out, and harried grad students scrambling to *just* finish everything, linger on campus burdened with mountains of exams to mark.

Charlotte stays late that night grading papers for Dr. O' Farrell. Time slips away from her, as it so often does while she is working. One of the frustrating things about grad school is the new relationship to time. Sometimes Charlotte finds herself thinking only minutes have passed only to look up and find it is hours later. Other times, time seemed still, an excruciating moment lasting eons. Either she has too much time on her hands or not enough of it. Either way, Charlotte feels like she doesn't know what she is doing.

Charlotte stumbles through the snow, a cardboard box full of the graded exams clutched to her chest, the corners digging into her uncomfortably. Her arms ache from the effort of carrying the overladen box. As she is the teaching assistant for a lecture of 200 undergrads she carries the weight of 200 scantrons, bubbles of graphite scribbled onto the circles of machine readable papers. Thankfully, their corresponding exam booklets are sitting in her office. She almost forgot that she has to hand in the scantrons before the office closes at 5:30pm. It is 5:00pm now, if she hurries and gets to the office in time, she will finally be done for the semester.

She still isn't sure that she *wants* to be done. With the semester. With working for Dr. O' Farrell.

She makes it to the scantron office with 10 minutes to spare, pushing the door open with her hip and making her way into the building backwards, grappling with the ungainly box in her arms. She manages to catch a smiling administrative assistant with a jaunty Christmas sweater before she locks up for the night. Gratefully, Charlotte sets the box down, pain tingling up her arms from its absence. The administrative assistant reaches over her desk and relieves Charlotte of her burden. The grey cubicle is made festive by shiny, green metallic tinsel and a matching shiny green tree that perches on the edge of her desk.

"There, I'm sure you're glad to be rid of that." The woman smiles. Charlotte smiles back. Even though the woman must have been itching to leave she makes smalltalk with Charlotte long enough for her freezing hands to begin to warm. Glancing at the clock and seeming to realize she is done for the day she says "Happy Holidays!"

Charlotte wishes her happy holidays in return and turns to leave. Venturing back outside, she feels the cold prickle over her skin, eyelids fluttering closed against the freezing wind, the icy air making her fingers stiffen. Relived of the awkward box, she can now plunge her hands into her pockets for extra warmth. She draws up her shoulders and braces herself against the onslaught.

The snow has been falling steadily all day and Charlotte has to wade through snowdrifts up to her ankles, the sidewalks have not yet been cleared. She can see her breath hang before her face in clouds of white that dissipate into the air. The campus is so quiet the silence unnerves her. She takes her earphones out of her pocket with shaking hands and turns something, anything on. An upbeat Christmas song starts playing. Good.

Charlotte always loved Christmas. Christmas songs, Christmas baking, Christmas decorations and how each one evoke their own memories. The song playing takes her to another place, away from the cold, lonely campus, to the living room, her brother and her standing on chairs and vying for the perfect spot to hang their decorations. Charlotte hums along as she makes her way through the snow.

Either she can continue on the straight path across the campus green, or, she can take a shortcut. It would certainly cut on time, however, even in the best weather the shortcut is dubbed the Death Stairs. As long as she takes her time down the steep steps she should be fine.

She cuts across the field to where a long and narrow staircase leads down the hill to Thornfield Hall. She puts one hand on the iron railing and starts to make the descent, concentrating on each step. There is absolutely no one in sight, she prays she won't fall.

A new song comes on. *City sidewalks, busy sidewalks dressed in holiday style, in the air there's a feeling of Christmas.*

Even though it is now December 20th, it does not feel like Christmas, not to Charlotte. Christmas meant bringing up the box of decorations from the basement on December 1st, it meant decorating the house with the knick knacks her family collected over the years. It meant Sunday visits from aunts and uncles and grandparents from out of town. But since the altercation at Thanksgiving, Charlotte has been excluded from all of that. December 20th is the day her family went to get the tree. They would make a whole day of it, driving down to the tree farm, tramping through the snow until they found the perfect one. They'd have hot chocolate while the tree was trussed up and tied to the roof of the car, then they would spend the evening decorating. They had gone without her of course. *It was Charlotte's choice to move away* her mom had said. *If she wanted to be here for this then she would be here.*

It is just like her mother to ignore the gesture of the house keys left in the mailbox. The message stating that Charlotte would not be back. This would be Charlotte's first Christmas on her own.

*Silver bells. Silver bells, it's Christmas time in the city. Hear them ring, ringaling-*

At that moment the clock tower at Emanuel Hall rings out in time to the song and Charlotte laughs. In her moment of distraction, her foot misses the step below her, her heel skidding along the slippery surface of the step below. Charlotte's leg shoots out from beneath her and she falls onto her hip. Here, beneath the vents of old Emanuel Hall the snow melted and refroze into a sheet of ice and Charlotte finds herself slipping over the steps, the corner of each step jarring painfully into her side. She scrambles to grab ahold of something, anything, so she can slow down, but she only comes away with fistfuls of snow. As she careens down the steps she screws her eyes shut, preparing herself for the pain of her sudden stop at the foot of the stairs. She should have stayed on the path.

Charlotte sails over the last three steps and soars into the air. She steels herself for the fall, praying she won't break anything. When she lands all the air leaves her lungs as she crashes to the ground. Reflexively, she throws out her hands to brace her fall, and one palm skids along the rough pavement and she can feel the tender skin of her palm tear. Charlotte holds her injured hand to her chest and lets the tears she suppressed all morning flow, her chest loosening.

She limps back to her office to get her things, eager to go home and put the day behind her. She is just reaching for her bag when a familiar form bursts through the door.

"I hope you weren't planning on leaving for the semester without saying goodbye Grey—fuck what happened! There's blood all over your sleeve." Dr. O' Farrell rushes over to her, his hands fluttering around her for a moment before he seems to come to his senses and he seizes her arm.

"I fell on the Death Stairs." She replies solemnly, her heart racing the moment his hands touch her own. He is holding her palm up to his face and scrutinizing it closely.

"I don't think you need stitches, but you definitely need to wrap this up. Have you washed the wound?"

"Have I washed the wound?" She repeats slowly. He gently drops her hand and peers into her face.

"You didn't hit your head too, did you?"

"No, just my hand."

    MEAGAN CLEVELAND

"Right. Come with me." Seizing her good hand in his, Dr. O' Farrell careens her down the empty hallway into his office. He steers her to her chair next to his desk and gently presses her into it. He turns around and drops behind his desk, disappearing from view.

"What are you doing?" Charlotte asks, raising herself slightly in her seat, trying to see.

"I know it's here somewhere," he mutters as he rummages around in his desk, or under his desk, Charlotte can't really tell what is going on over there.

"Aha!"

Dr. O' Farrell pops up from behind his desk bearing a red case.

"First aid kit." He announces triumphantly. He comes around the desk and perches on the edge as he wrestles the case open and dumps out the contents. He selects sanitizer, gauze and tape and gets to work.

Gently he takes hold of Charlotte's injured hand and turns her palm upwards and surveys the cut with sympathy. He tears open the sanitizing wipes and disinfects the wound. Once the dried blood is scrubbed away he presses a square of gauze over the wound and tapes it in place.

"There. That will do for now."

"Thank you."

"Anything for you, Grey." He says gruffly, still holding on to her bandaged hand.

"So." Charlotte begins. "Why were you looking for me?"

"Right. I completely forgot. I realize the semester has ended and Christmas holidays have begun. But I know that you will not be merry, after that big fight with your mum at

Thanksgiving. Did you have any plans for the holiday?" He asks, his grip on her hand tightening slightly. She winces and he lets go. "Sorry! Sorry!"

"It's okay." She holds her bandaged hand to her chest. "No, I don't have any plans. Beyond doing some reading for my winter courses."

"Bollocks." He scoffs. "You won't have time for reading. Not now." He grins.

"Not now?" She repeats.

He peers at her with mock concern.

"You sure you didn't hit your head, Grey?"

She shakes her head in response.

"I would have thought it was obvious, that you'd be welcome round at mine for Christmas."

"Really?" She breathes, a smile stretching across her face. He smiles in return.

"Really! I was hoping you didn't have plans. How about you come over on Christmas Eve? I'll get your room ready."

Her heart skips a beat when he says the words *your room*.

"That sound great!" She rises from the chair and he narrows his eyes at her.

"Where do you think you're going?"

"I better go Christmas shopping."

"Not tonight. You've had a bad fall. Tonight you rest. Tomorrow we'll go shopping."

"We?"

"Well yeah," he grins at her. "I need to get your present."

 

# CHAPTER TWENTY

## DONUM

It is Christmas Eve. Charlotte stands before the door, her hand raised over the knocker. At her side sits a small suitcase and bags laden with gifts and baked goods.

She gnaws at her lip. She has looked forward to this, filling her days with a flurry of activity to try to make the time go by faster. She met Dr. O' Farrell downtown and they walked among twinkling lights with hot chocolate in hand, only parting ways to get gifts for one another. She wasn't sure what to get him until she saw it in a speciality shop window. A model car, a black Lexus. To replace the one she 'destroyed' the day they met. She bites down a laugh at the thought of his face when he opens the gift. The image gives her strength. She raises her hand once more to knock but her fist meets empty air. The door has already opened.

Dr. O' Farrell stands in the doorway in a holiday sweater, a great grin plastered on his face.

"How long did you plan to stand out there?" He laughs.

She blushes and reaches for her bags.

"Come now, Grey. You know that's my job." He protests, reaching over her to grab her suitcase and the largest of her bags. "You can get the little one."

"Alright." She laughs and follows him inside.

The house feels like it has awakened from its enchanted slumber. It is no longer cold and inaccessible, but warm, the air scented with cinnamon, cloves, and pine. Garlands of fresh greenery are draped over the doorways, twinkling golden lights and sparkling golden glass balls are threaded through the branches. A nine foot tall tree sits in the living room, suffusing the room with its golden light.

"It looks beautiful." She breathes in awe. Dr. O' Farrell looks over his shoulder with a soft smile.

"Anything for you, Grey." He clears his throat and looks away. "I'll take these things upstairs and meet you in the kitchen?"

"Wait! Give me that bag please, there are some things in there I should put in the kitchen." He passes her the bag and makes his way upstairs.

Charlotte watches him go up the stairs then walks into the living room towards the tree. She reaches into the bag and takes out a small box wrapped in shining green and gold paper and delicately places it under the tree. Smiling, she hurries into the kitchen and starts to unload her bags.

She feels Dr. O' Farrell's presence when he walks quietly into the room. But he does not stay quiet for long.

"Good god, Grey. Did you rob a bakery?" He asks, peering over her shoulder at the plates she has set out.

"No." She turns around to face him with a smile. "I made them."

"You made them? For me?"

She nods.

Not taking his eyes away from her face, he leans towards her. She holds her breath when his face comes closer to her

 MEAGAN CLEVELAND

own, but she feels his arm brush past hers and laughs. He pops a shortbread cookie in his mouth and groans.

"This is fucking delicious. Who taught you to bake?"

"My grandmother."

"Thank you grandma."

She laughs again and the two of them pack plates with Christmas baking while the tea steeps.

In between mouthfuls of food Charlotte asks, "So what is the plan?"

"The food is coming tonight. We can eat what we want and have the leftovers tomorrow?" Charlotte nods in a approval. "After dinner I thought we could finish decorating the tree? Then maybe we could sing some carols?"

"Carols?" She raises a brow.

"I like Christmas carols." He grumbles. "We don't have to do it."

"No, I think it will be fun."

"Good."

They enjoy their catered dinner and hang gold and silver ornaments on the tree and, they do indeed go carolling. Charlotte finds herself a little embarrassed but when Dr. O' Farrell begins to sing all her anxiety melts away and they lose themselves in the music. Soon it is late and they make their way home while snow gently drifts down from the clouds.

"Well, off to bed with you or Father Christmas won't come." Dr. O' Farrell winks at her.

Charlotte laughs. "Did you sneak some whiskey into your hot chocolate?"

"Maybe."

They make their way up the stairs together. Charlotte avoids looking at the wedding photo as she passes, but she swears she can feel Antoinette O'Farrell's eyes follow her down the hall.

"Goodnight. Thanks for such a wonderful day." Charlotte beams up at Dr. O' Farrell.

"Goodnight, Charlotte." He leans down and brushes his lips across her forehead. She closes her eyes at his touch. When she opens her eyes he is gone.

It is Christmas morning. Charlotte wakes early, feeling like a child bursting with excitement. She pulls a sweater over her pyjamas and pads out of the bedroom and down the hallway. Dr. O' Farrell's door is open. She peeks her head inside. He is not in his room. He must be downstairs.

She does her best not to rush down the stairs. The house twinkles with golden fairy lights, the smell of cinnamon wafting from the kitchen. Dr. O' Farrell sits at the kitchen table sipping at a cup of tea.

"Merry Christmas," Charlotte calls out.

He raises his cup. "Happy Christmas. There's tea in the pot if you want some."

While Charlotte pours herself a cup, a timer goes off and Dr. O' Farrell pulls cinnamon buns out of the oven. After breakfast the two head into the living room. Presents are stacked beneath the tree and the sight brings a small burst of pain to Charlotte. She thinks of her family sitting around their own tree.

     MEAGAN CLEVELAND

Charlotte pulls her phone out of her pocket and texts her brother. She vows to give him a call later that day.

She looks up to find Dr. O' Farrell's eyes on her.

"Messaging your brother?"

Charlotte nods.

"Good. Well, would you care to open a present?"

The two of them sit cross legged on the floor next to the tree. Charlotte grabs the green and gold present and passes it to Dr. O' Farrell.

"You first."

"If you insist." He grins, tearing at the paper. He looks down and barks out a laugh.

"Is this?"

"A new car. To make up for the one I wrecked." Charlotte smiles as he sets the model car on the coffee table.

"That's hilarious." He wipes a tear from his eye and reaches for a large present under the tree wrapped in red paper. He passes it over to her with a smile.

Charlotte carefully tears the paper to reveal the gift underneath.

"Trivial Pursuit?"

"The latest edition. This way, when we play later today you won't cheat." He smiles at her.

She looks down at the present, her eyes filling with tears.

"Ah, don't be daft, Grey!" He sits up and scoots closer to her, wrapping an arm around her shoulders. "We've got our holiday tradition to uphold."

She looks up at him and beams, throwing her arms around his neck. He sags a little beneath the force of her embrace and chuckles.

Their faces are close, too close, his lips brush across her cheeks, a promise begging to be kept.

She draws away and looks up at the ceiling.

"Look." She whispers.

He looks up and they both go quiet.

"Mistletoe."

They look at each other.

Time stills.

Charlotte is keenly aware of her chest pressed against his, their hearts beating as one. Her eyes flicker from his brown eyes to his lips. He inhales sharply and closes the distance between them.

The kiss is like coming home. The moment his lips touch hers Charlotte feels warmth well up inside her. His hand goes to the back of her head, tilting it back to deepen the kiss. Charlotte sighs and his kisses become more urgent, more hungry. When his lips leave hers she wants to cry out in protest but he does not stop, instead pressing his lips to her hair, her forehead, her cheeks, until finally, he covers her lips with his own once more.

"You have no idea how long I've wanted to do that." He gasps.

"Oh yes I do."

They laugh, the sound of their laughter masking the sound of a car pulling up in the driveway. A figure emerges and heads for the door.

# CHAPTER TWENTY ONE

## HOSPES

Charlotte is leaning in for another kiss when there is a knock at the door. D. O'Farrell frowns in confusion for a moment until horror leaches the colour from his face.

"Fuck!" He claps a hand over his mouth to muffle the outburst. "I forgot to tell her not to come."

"Who?" Charlotte asks, confused at the sudden change in him.

Dr. O' Farrell jumps up just as a key turns in the lock.

Charlotte looks at him in disbelief. Whoever he is expecting has their own key.

The door opens and cold wind heralds the entrance of a woman Charlotte has never seen.

She is in her sixties or seventies, her platinum hair cut in an elegant bob. Her lips are a vibrant red, at odds with her pale complexion. She is wearing an oversized pair of sunglasses, the type Jackie Kennedy would favour. She raises the glasses from the bridge of her nose and stares at Dr. O' Farrell.

"Am I interrupting?" She drawls.

Dr. O' Farrell approaches the woman and gives her a brisk kiss on the cheek.

"This is Charlotte. She is my...friend. Charlotte, this is Mrs. Mason. My mother-in-law."

The two women trade looks of cold appraisal.

So this was Antoinette's mother. The woman who hijacks every holiday and turns the occasion into a never-ending wake for her daughter. Though she bears no love for the woman, Charlotte resolves to be polite. She rises to her feet and holds out a hand.

"Nice to meet you."

Mrs. Mason looks at the proffered hand and sniffs. She brushes past Charlotte and into the house. She does not take Charlotte's hand.

Dr. O' Farrell turns to Charlotte, his eyes pleading.

"I'm so sorry." He says hoarsely, his voice lowered so as not to alert his unwanted guest. "There is no reason for her to be so rude to you."

"I can think of a reason." Charlotte murmurs, her eyes travelling up the stairs to where the portrait of his dead wife hangs.

He looks down at his rumpled pyjamas and hastily tied bathrobe. He looks at Charlotte in her own pyjamas and swears.

"Fuck. She's going to get the wrong idea."

Charlotte raises a brow.

His cheeks redden.

"Don't look at me like that. You know what I mean. I don't want her to think we spent the night together."

"We did spend the night together."

He turns a more vibrant shade of red, the colour spreading to his ears and neck.

     **MEAGAN CLEVELAND**

"Not in the same bed we didn't." He replies through gritted teeth.

Charlotte's stomach plummets. Oh. It did look bad.

"I'll go get dressed." She says flatly, passing him without looking at him and rushing up the stairs.

She pulls on a green knit dress and pulls her hair back. She pauses in from of the mirror, raising her hands to her face and tracing her lips with her fingertips. Minutes before she was *kissing* him. She has never felt like this, she should be happy, should be ecstatic that he shares her feelings. While her lips still feel the ghost of his touch, she feels oddly hollow. It must be because of Mrs. Mason's intrusion.

She takes her time making her way back downstairs, following the sound of lowered voices into the kitchen.

Mrs. Mason stands with her arms crossed, a frown marring her face. Dr. O' Farrell looms over her, gesturing wildly while he speaks. Mrs. Mason's eyes dart from her shoes over towards Charlotte, her frown deepening. Dr. O' Farrell whirls around to face her.

"We'll be just a few minutes."

His dismissal cuts her.

"Oh. Okay. I'll go clear up the mess in the living room." She replies, ducking her head to hide the tears that flood her eyes. She wipes furiously at her face. She shouldn't be upset. This is his house. If he needs privacy it's his right.

She surveys the mess of wrapping paper and ribbons littering the room and realizes that she does not have a garbage bag. She does not want to head back into the kitchen so she decides the next rational place to search for garbage bags and other cleaning supplies would be the basement.

She heads the the staircase and stands before the closed door. She grasps the doorknob and turns, exhaling as the door swings open without a sound. She gazes into the darkness beyond and bites her lip. She didn't want Dr. O' Farrell to think she was snooping. She is just trying to be helpful. She steels her shoulders, flicks on the lights and makes the descent.

She is secretly pleased to see that Antoinette O'Farrell had not got round to decorating the basement. The basement looks exactly as you would expect a basement to look: poorly lit, unfinished and chock full of storage boxes. Leaning against a wall is a metal set of shelves bearing cleaning supplies, garbage bags and toilet paper. Charlotte silently applauds her intuition and reaches for the black bags when she spots something out of the corner of her eye. A storage bin, the lid slightly askew. Written on the side of the box is the name *Antoinette.*

Charlotte hovers beside the box, fighting an inner battle with herself. But curiosity wins out. She nudges the lid aside and looks within. Inside are scores of leather-bound journals. Charlotte frowns. Dr. O' Farrell kept her diaries?

Just as she is reaching within the box, she hears a voice from upstairs.

"I'll see you out." Dr. O' Farrell's voice is uncharacteristically loud.

Charlotte drops her hand to her sides and straightens.

She rushes up the stairs.

And one of the journals is missing from the pile.

Charlotte hides the journal in the pocket of her winter coat which hangs in the hallway.

Finally, the sharp staccato of Mrs. Mason's heels are interrupted by the creaking of the front door. Charlotte holds her breath as she listens to the soft thud of the door closing, the click of the locks that are turned in place.

Just as she is turning around, Dr. O' Farrell appears at her side, his hands fluttering beside him like pale birds as he apologizes.

"I'm so sorry Charlotte. I know it was terribly rude of me to shut you out of the conversation but I knew she wanted to talk to me alone—"

"It's fine." Charlotte interrupts. Closing her eyes so he does not detect the glimmer of tears there. Not from sadness but frustration.

"I'm so sorry."

"It's okay." Charlotte answers automatically.

"No. It isn't. She was rude to you."

He steps closer to her and she leans into his warmth.

He looks down.

"You look nice." He smiles. Then he steps away, a draft of cold air settling between them. "Look at me. Still in my nightclothes. I better get dressed. Wait for me?"

Charlotte smiles. "I'll put the kettle on."

"Good girl."

Charlotte blushes and heads towards the kitchen.

Once he is gone she heaves a sigh. She takes the kettle off the stove, fills it with water, and sets it back into place. She turns the burner on and waits.

Her mind drifts to the journal. She can't believe she has

taken it. There isn't time to put it back now, she'd have to find some excuse to go back to the basement later.

She is so lost in thought she does not register the shrill whistle from the stove beside her until an arm brushes past her to shut it off.

"Earth to Charlotte." Dr. O' Farrell says playfully as he pours the boiling water into the teapot. He glances at her face and frowns. "Everything okay?"

"Yeah."

He sets the teapot down with a dull thud.

"I'm sorry. You must be missing your family."

"Yes." She lies. Anything to change the topic.

"Is there anything I can do to help?" He asks earnestly.

She smiles weakly in reply.

"I'll take a cup of tea please."

Grinning, he stirs a teaspoon of sugar and a dash of milk into her cup then pours the steeped tea overtop.

She takes the cup from him, the heat of the tea scalding her hands. But she doesn't notice. She is thinking of the journal hidden in her coat pocket.

# CHAPTER TWENTY TWO

## TEMPESTAS

That evening there is a storm. The grey clouds pregnant with the promise of snow unloose their burden at last. Fat white flakes fall in quick succession, stirred up by viscous winds until the sky is completely white.

The day is utterly ruined. Dr. O' Farrell and Charlotte sit in awkward silence while scores of saccharine Christmas films fill the quiet between them.

Charlotte stands at the window, her eyes on the snow but her mind drifts back to her discovery in the basement. Humiliated by the arrival of Mrs. Mason, Charlotte is desperate to retreat to her room to peruse the journal.

"Why don't we go back into the living room? We can open up the Trivial Pursuit."

She shakes her head.

"I'm tired. I think I'll head up to bed."

There is a beat of silence. It stretches out awkwardly between them.

"Okay." He sighs, rubbing his hand up the back of his neck.

Where her own hands had been not so long ago.

"Goodnight." Charlotte utters the word without looking

at him, turning on her heel and heading up the stairs. On the way up she grabs her coat.

Once in her room she hangs the coat in the wardrobe, the material pulled to one side by the weight of the journal. She quickly changes into her pyjamas and tiptoes across the hardwood until she is standing before the wardrobe. Gingerly, she reaches into the pocket and withdraws the leather bound journal. She tiptoes back across to the bed and slips under the covers. Holding her breath she slowly opens the journal, the whisper of the pages against her fingertips the only sound.

Charlotte leafs through pages and pages of notes, notes all about paintings of the High Renaissance. While she resents the neat and looping script of Antoinette O'Farrell at first, soon she comes to forget the ghost of her long dead rival and comes to form a kinship with another scholar. Antoinette's notes are concise, thought provoking. The more she reads the more she comes to know the enigmatic woman, a woman with a deep knowledge and passion for her subject, a woman who surely would have gone places if her life had not been cut tragically short. No wonder Mrs. Mason looked on her with such loathing, her, living the life that her daughter should be living.

As she reads, the ideas presented by Antoinette start to seem familiar, especially a particular phrase. She sets the journal aside and reaches for her laptop. After opening the Thornfield library website she types in the name Ellis O' Farrell. And there— the same phrase from Antoinette O'Farrell's personal journal appears in an article by Dr. O' Farrell. She downloads the article and begins to read.

After what seems like an eternity, she eases back into her pillows, the words floating in her mind's eye. She finishes

     MEAGAN CLEVELAND

the lengthy article, paying close attention to the footnotes, the bibliography, the acknowledgments. No mention on Antoinette. None at all.

She reaches for the journal, opening it at the page she marked with a ribbon. She flips back a few pages to the date of that entry. It is from fifteen years ago.

She reaches for her laptop, opening up the article and going to the citation information. The article was printed ten years ago. After Antoinette O'Farrell died.

It couldn't be. Ellis O'Farrell couldn't have stolen his late wife's research, couldn't have passed it off as his own.

Yet. The evidence is staring her straight in the face. There is no denying the age of the journal, the pages yellowed by the sun, the corners worn smoothing by searching fingers.

Dr. Ellis O'Farrell, her one friend, her mentor, the one who made her heart race—is a thief and a liar.

There is only one question Charlotte needs answered.

What does he want with her?

Charlotte lays awake in her bed that night. She watches the shadows that pace outside her door, the figure behind it silent and watchful. She listens to the howling wind, the scrape of hail against the windows. She feels the cold creeping up her fingertips to ice her cheeks, her chin, the pointed tip of her nose. Soon the heavy shadows weighted with secrets smother her to sleep.

When she wakes the next morning, her breath hovers before her face in a small cloud. She reaches for the light switch and flicks it on, but nothing happens. The power is out. She rubs her hands together then holds them to her face, breathing into her cupped palms. She dresses quickly, layering a tank and t-shirt beneath her knitted sweater and rolling a second pair of socks onto her feet. As she heads to the door of her bedroom she pauses by the window. The world outside is covered with a thick blanket of snow, fat flakes still drifting down relentlessly. She squints as she thinks she sees the shadow of a figure beneath the one of the large oak trees outside, but the image soon disappears. Shaking her head, Charlotte reaches for the door and pauses as her discovery from the night before flashes in her mind.

What should she say to Dr. O' Farrell? Should she say anything at all? Should she confront him? Give him the benefit of the doubt? A chance to explain himself?

Gnawing at her lip, she turns from the door and heads back to her bed and reaches for the journal where it sits on her nightstand. Its pages fall open to where she left off last night, Antoinette's neat handwriting standing in stark relief from the yellowing pages.

As she stands there, deciding on the best course of action, a knock sounds at her door. Charlotte freezes. the journal in her hand like a hot brand.

"Breakfast. Come down once you are dressed." Dr O'Farrell's voice cheerfully calls from the other side of the closed door.

Charlotte heaves a sigh of relief, thrusting the journal underneath her pillow and making sure that it is out of sight before she leaves her room.

Growing up, Boxing Day was always a day of relaxation. The big day finally over, the family could spend some well deserved rest eating leftovers and enjoying the gifts of the day before.

Today, Charlotte feels anything but relaxed. She is on edge, she sits stiffly in her chair as Dr. O' Farrell passes her a bowl of cereal. Charlotte eats the food mechanically but does not taste it. Anxiety churns her stomach. Her mind keeps going back to her discovery of the night before and she finds that she cannot bring herself to look the professor in the eyes.

"Sorry about breakfast. I had planned to do a fry up with scrambled eggs, buttered toast, baked beans, crispy bacon, the lot, but the power's out."

Charlotte shrugs and spoons the bland cereal into her mouth. She is just raising another spoonful to her lips when she feels the weight of Dr. O' Farrell's gaze. He is staring at her. The spoon hovers before her face.

"Is anything the matter?" She asks.

"I should be asking you that." Dr. O' Farrell replies. "You are very quiet this morning."

"Just tired."

"Did you have trouble sleeping last night?"

She nods and shoves the spoon into her mouth, hoping to quell any further questions. Thankfully, Dr. O' Farrell takes the hint, he remains silent as he clears her half-eaten bowl and takes it over to the sink. Charlotte takes her chance and slips out of the kitchen and into the living room.

As she cleared up all the wrapping paper yesterday there is no cleaning to be done. No busy work to occupy her restless hands. Instead she settles on the antique chaise and stares out at the storm. Snow flakes dance outside the window, the sky almost completely white. Snow drifts as high as her waist have piled up alongside the house. It would not be so easy to take her leave.

Charlotte bites her lip. She does not know what she should do. Surely she cannot spend another minute with a man who has lied to her, but how can she leave? She knows she should confront him about the journal, but the thought of starting an argument she cannot escape from makes her heart thud in her chest.

Growing up, Charlotte always avoided arguments at all costs. Her parents constantly argued until the day her father left. She hoped his absence would mean the absence of her mother's vitriol but she was wrong. Without her father in the house her mother turned her critical eye towards Charlotte. Rather than stand up for herself or fight back, Charlotte let herself be the target for her mother's rage, hoping she could keep Geoff out of range.

All those years of staying silent, of putting up with the worst, make Charlotte wish to simply forget her discovery, to pretend that all is well. But she doesn't know how to look at Dr. O' Farrell now.

He isn't the man she thought he was.

*Thud.*

Charlotte starts when she hears the noise. It seems to be coming from the basement. She pads across the floor to the basement door which stands ajar. Did Dr. O' Farrell go downstairs?

"What are you doing?"

Charlotte leaps back from the door and whips around. Dr. O' Farrell is standing behind her, obviously having come from the kitchen. But if he is here, who is downstairs?

"I thought, I thought I heard something down there." Charlotte stammers.

"It's just you and me." He smiles.

Dr. O' Farrell steps closer to her, his arm brushing past her to close the basement door behind her. He stands with his back to her for a moment.

"I'd rather you not go down there. It's a bit of a mess."

Charlotte knows for a fact the basement is neatly organized. Why doesn't he want her to go down there? She already knows his secret.

*But he doesn't know that.*

They spend the rest of the day in an uncomfortable silence. They both sit in the living room, wrapped in a blanket, doing some reading. Though she has a book open on her lap Charlotte has not read a thing, her eyes remain unfocused on the page as her mind races. *What should she do? What should she say?*

Every now and then Dr. O' Farrell looks up from his book to cast Charlotte a worried glance but she ignores it. She is not ready to initiate a conversation.

Charlotte is angry. Her uncertain future with Dr. O' Farrell is daunting to say the least and the revelation that he is keeping secrets from her is a blow. As angry and confused as she is, she is not ready to confront him, not yet. She needs time to think over her discovery before she tells him that she knows, and then he would explain himself and everything would be alright again. Wouldn't it?

Day turns to evening and the airy house darkens considerably. Dr. O' Farrell abandons his armchair to find some candles and place them throughout the room. It should be romantic, together alone in the candlelight. But Charlotte is uneasy, the candlelight casting long flickering shadows on the walls, each glimmer of movement making her start.

"What is the matter?" Dr. O' Farrell finally demands. Charlotte opens her mouth to speak when he curtly interrupts, "And don't you dare say 'nothing,' Grey."

Charlotte swallows the words. The reappearance of her surname like an arrow to the heart.

Dr. O' Farrell rises from his chair to kneel before her, his face softened in the candlelight. Charlotte feels her resolve waver, only to look at the large, dark shadow he has cast behind him and she steels herself against him.

"Why does something have to be the matter? I am just a quiet person."

He frowns at her answer, a wounded expression on his face.

"I know you are quiet. But you've never frozen me out like this before. You've always said what was on your mind. What's on your mind, Grey?"

Charlotte groans in exasperation.

"I just don't feel like talking." She replies through gritted teeth.

Dr. O' Farrell straightens and makes his way back to his armchair across the room, trying, and failing, to hide the look of disappointment on his face.

For a moment Charlotte feels guilty. Then she remembers the journal.

She shuts the book on her lap. He looks up at her.

"I'm going to bed."

As she storms up the stairs she hears his voice call quietly up after her.

"Goodnight, Charlotte."

She hurries into her room and shuts the door behind her. She does not bother to undress but hops into the bed and pulls up the covers. Sleep soon finds her.

But she does not sleep for long.

She wakes with a start. Sleep clouds her mind and for a moment she struggles to identify her surroundings. Realization floods her. She is in Dr. O' Farrell's house. Dr. O' Farrell. The thief. The liar.

Her eyes snap open. Darkness envelops her. Soon her eyes grow accustomed to the dark and she is alarmed to find a patch of shadow darker than the rest.

A figure looms over her, an outstretched hand feeling its way through the night.

She sits up, brandishing her phone so that its light illuminates the room. The figure throws its hands up before its face, shielding itself from the sudden glare. Charlotte recognizes the pale hair.

"Adele?"

Slowly, the figure lowers its hands.

It isn't Adele.

It is Blanche.

"Blanche, what are you doing here?" Charlotte whispers, rising from the bed to approach the other young woman.

Blanche sneers at her.

"What am I doing here? What are you doing here? What could he possibly want with you?"

Though Charlotte asked herself the very same thing not too long ago, she bristles against the insult.

"We're friends." Charlotte crosses her arms over her chest, hunches her shoulders inward. Makes herself small.

"Whatever, I don't care. Give me that journal." Blanche reaches for the book but Charlotte snatches it up.

"What do you want with it?"

"None of your business. Give it to me."

"No."

Clutching the journal to her chest, Charlotte takes a step back.

Blanche takes a step forward.

"Give it to me. Now."

Blanche lunges forward, grabbing the journal with vengeful hands, her nails raking across Charlotte's arms.

"No!" Charlotte cries, holding the journal closer, ducking her head against Blanche's blows. The two stumble into the side table, the lamp crashing to the ground.

They pause.

Light floods through the crack beneath the door. A shadow pauses on the other side.

"Charlotte? Are you alright?"

Charlotte opens her mouth to reply when a hand slaps over her face, covering her mouth. Charlotte's cries are muffled against Blanche's palm. But Charlotte will not be silenced. She draws back her arm and hurls the journal across the room. It hits the door with a sickening thud.

The doorknob rattles and the door swings open, Dr. O' Farrell barrels into the room. He pulls up short at the sight of the two women.

"Blanche?" He utters in disbelief.

"Ellis." Blanche flashes a grimace at the professor, her hand still gripping Charlotte's wrist, hard.

"Blanche, what are you doing? We've been through this before. You can't just keep showing up at the house like this."

While Blanche is distracted Charlotte breaks free, backing away from the other woman.

"Thanksgiving. That was you in my room!" Charlotte gasps.

Blanche whips around, her eyes blazing with fury.

"Your room? A few years ago this was my room. Back then he was trying to get into my pants, and once he did he got into my head as well." She whips away from Charlotte to face Dr. O' Farrell.

"Wasn't I enough for you? Wasn't Antoinette? Now her too—"

"That's enough. I told you last time I wouldn't press charges. But you are scaring me, Blanche. I think it's time to call the police."

He steps forward, grabs hold of Blanche's arm and propels her forwards, towards the door. But Blanche digs in her heels. She will not be moved.

"It's too late." Blanche says. "She knows."

"What are you talking about?" Dr. O' Farrell snaps, his grip on her arm tightening.

"She. Knows." Blanche repeats. Then she nods towards the journal lying on the floor by the door.

Dr.O'Farrell follows her gaze. When he sees the journal his face pales. He drops Blanche's arm as he turns towards Charlotte.

"Charlotte. I can explain."

# CHAPTER TWENTY THREE

## PROELIUM

"Charlotte. Please let me explain." Dr. O' Farrell repeats, his tone pleading.

"I think it's pretty simple." Charlotte calmly replies. "Antoinette's notes predate your article. By all accounts it looks like you've taken credit for her work."

Dr. O' Farrell stumbles back as if struck by a blow.

"Charlotte. You can't think that I—"

"What else is she supposed to think? Wait till you hear the title of his next article. An article she practically wrote, an article which does not give her *any* credit as co-author. You see? This is what he does, collects pretty young women, leeches their ideas, their minds until they are of no more use to him and he tosses them aside. Women like me. At least I'm still alive, not like Antoinette—"

"Shut your mouth about Antoinette. You don't know anything about it." He growls. But Blanche does not flinch.

"Please. I know more than you think. I found all your boxes in the basement. Years worth of research to plunder. I wonder what dear old Mrs. Mason would think about all this?"

Dr. O' Farrell's pale skin flushes an angry scarlet.

"How dare you. First you break into my home, then you threaten to harass my grieving family—"

"Some way to treat a grieving woman. To steal from her dearly departed daughter and not cut her in on any share of your earnings."

"You know nothing, *nothing*, about it!"

"Enough!" Charlotte cries out. The two pause to stare at her. It is as if they have forgotten she is even there.

"You are both as bad as the other. Now, get out of my room!" Charlotte pushes the two figures out of the room and slams the door. Turns the lock.

A fist pounds against the closed door but Charlotte ignores it. Breathing heavily she ignores the yells and shouts in the hallway as she pulls out her suitcase. She grabs all her clothes from the wardrobe and shoves them in the suitcase, slamming it closed.

For a moment she stands in the centre of the room, considering what to do. She knows what she wants to do, she wants to run back to Dr. O' Farrell and find comfort in his arms. She wants to hide from the truth and what that might mean for her and Dr. O' Farrell's relationship. If what they have is a real relationship.

Finally coming to a decision, she hastily pulls on her coat, unlocks and opens the door.

Dr. O' Farrell has his back turned to her as he grapples with Blanche. He seems to be trying to compel her to leave but Blanche will not budge.

Charlotte rushes past them and hurries down the stairs, stuffing her feet into her boots as she comes to the door.

"Charlotte! Charlotte! Wait, *please*!" Dr. O' Farrell's desperate cries trail behind her. She opens the front door, steps outside and slams it behind her.

She treads through the snow until she cannot hear the sound of his voice any longer.

It turns out that one cannot drag a heavy suitcase behind oneself in a snowdrift very easily, if not at all. The snow is now at her underarms. She cannot carry her suitcase under her arm, but must try to carry it over her head. Soon her arms begin to quake and she needs to rest.

She kicks a spot clear of snow and sets her suitcase down and then collapses on top of it. Each breath is like inhaling shards of glass. Snowflakes continue to fall. It is dark and Charlotte can only see a wide expanse of white. She does not know where the road is.

Her arms and legs aching, she resolves to wait for another five minutes. Those five minutes become ten, the ten become twenty and Charlotte finds it difficult to keep her eyes open. Her eyes flutter open and closed as the snow piles up around her. She shivers against the chill.

But soon she can not feel anything at all.

By the time Charlotte regains feeling in her limbs she is no longer in the snow.

She is not sure where she is.

She can hear shrill whistles and monotonous beeps, muffled whispers and sudden bouts of laughter. She is distantly aware that she is in pain somewhere, but it is difficult to tell. She almost feels as if she is floating, the pain a distant island she is swimming away from. Her hands feel heavy, strange. She finds it difficult to open her eyes but manages to peel them open. She immediately closes them against the bright glare of florescent lights.The monotonous beeping increases its tempo and soon Charlotte can hear the sound of approaching footsteps.

"Good, you're awake."

Charlotte tries to squint towards the voice but cannot look into the glare of lights.

"Oh, let me get that for you."

The lights dim and finally Charlotte can open her eyes. She is in a hospital. Her hands are wrapped in bandages. The figure standing in front of her is a nurse dressed in bright scrubs. The nurse reaches for her chart and starts to ask a flurry of questions. What is your name? Date of birth? Do you know what day it is? So on and so forth until Charlotte's head begins to ache. The nurse notices her grimace.

"You okay? When your friend found you in the snow you were just beginning to show signs of frostnip."

"Frostnip?" Charlotte repeats.

"Yep. Frostnip. A milder form of frostbite. Though some of your fingers do show signs of superficial frostbite. I'm afraid it did start to blister. The doctor will be in soon okay?"

Charlotte nods. When the doctor does arrive she gives Charlotte a prescription for antibiotics and recommends Charlotte take over the counter pain relief if needed. As quickly as she arrives the doctor departs.

The nurse returns some time later to discharge her, helping Charlotte to dress in her coat.

"Your friend is in the waiting room."

Friend? Dr. O' Farrell's face flashes in her mind, a stab of pain in her chest accompanies the image. Charlotte walks slowly out of the emergency room and into the waiting room. There, an unexpected figure is waiting for her.

"Joanna?"

Joanna is standing in the waiting room, swaying gently on her feet, her eyes lowered to the phone in her hand. She looks up as Charlotte steps through the sliding doors, a wrinkle between her brows. She glances at Charlotte's bandaged hands.

"Okay?"

Charlotte nods. She looks around, panic riding in her throat. "My suitcase—"

"It's in my car. I found it next to you in the snow. Come on." She jerks her head and holds out an arm. Charlotte approaches her warily, not expecting the other girl to wrap her arm around her shoulders. "I'll take you home."

The two walk in silence down the brightly lit hospital corridors, twisting and turning their way down the long, colourless, hallways until they are out in the parking lot.

The cold wind hits Charlotte's cheeks like a slap and within her bandages her fingertips begin to burn. Charlotte whimpers and Joanna tightens her grip on her shoulders.

"We're just over here. Not too far to go."

It really isn't far but Charlotte is in agony each step. Outside the shelter of the hospital entrance, the wind whips the girls' hair to a frenzy, snowflakes blast into their faces like needles. Each breath feels like a knife to the chest, her hands soon become numb to the cold. Finally they reach Joanna's car. Joanna opens the door for Charlotte, helps her with her seatbelt and shuts the door firmly before going to the driver's seat. She starts the car, heat floods from the vents and Charlotte whimpers again as she regains feeling in her fingers.

"They give you anything for pain?"

Charlotte shakes her head. "Just antibiotics. The doctor said to take ibuprofen or acetaminophen if it hurts."

"Asshole." Joanna mutters darkly.

"The doctor was a woman."

"Bitch then."

Joanna reaches down for the long wooden brush down the side of the door. She jumps out of the car and quickly brushes the snow from the windows and mirrors before hopping back inside.

"So, where to?"

Charlotte bites her lip. She longs for the warmth and familiarity of Dr. O' Farrell's house but quickly remembers why that is not an option. Swallowing back tears she gives Joanna her address.

The disconnected, floating feeling from the hospital is gone. Instead Charlotte is very much grounded by her pain, a searing heat in her fingers that intensifies the warmer the car becomes. The pain in her hands is nothing compared to the heartache she feels.

She should be sitting in front of the Christmas tree, in Dr. O' Farrell's arms. But instead she is here, with Joanna of all people.

They drive in silence, the bright headlights of oncoming cars burn into Charlotte's eyes. She closes them and tilts her head back.

Suddenly the car stops. Charlotte opens her eyes and turns her head to look at Joanna.

"You fell asleep. You okay?"

"Yeah." Charlotte goes to undo her seatbelt, then remembers she cannot with her bandaged hands.

"Let me."

Joanna hops out of the car and opens Charlotte's door, unbuckles her seat belt and helps her out of the car. While Charlotte stands there, blinking against the cold, Joanna opens the trunk and withdraws Charlotte's suitcase.

"Keys?" Joanna asks.

"Front pocket."

Joanna fishes out the keys and heads for the door to the apartment building. She holds it open with her hip and Charlotte slips through the doorway.

"We have to go up the stairs."

Joanna sighs but picks up the suitcase without a word and follows Charlotte up the staircase.

Charlotte steps into her apartment and sees the miniature tree on her coffee table and can't stop the flood of tears that escape down her cheeks. Joanna rolls the suitcase into the small living room then turns to face Charlotte.

"Will you be okay by yourself? You want me to stay the night?"

Charlotte looks at her incredulously.

"Why are you being so nice to me?" She stammers through tears.

"Don't get too used to it. Once you are feeling better you and I are going to have a serious talk about what exactly you were doing at Dr. O' Farrell's house."

The sound of his name makes her cry even harder. Joanna sighs again and wraps an arm around Charlotte's shoulders and steers her to the bedroom. After insisting she can change her own clothes Charlotte nudges the bedroom door closed and struggles to put on her nightclothes.

While she undresses she can hear Joanna rummaging around the kitchen cupboards, the doors opening and closing with a crack. The kettle begins to shriek. Charlotte does not understand why Joanna is helping her but she is fiercely glad of the other girl's company.

There is a knock at her bedroom door.

"Come in."

Joanna enters with two steaming mugs of tea. She sets them down on the nightstand and sits cross legged on Charlotte's bed.

"So. Sleepover?"

While they wait for the tea to cool Joanna demands Charlotte tell her exactly what has been going on between her and Dr. O' Farrell. She explains her loneliness, Dr. O' Farrell's kindness, the friendship between them and how it blossomed into something more.

"So nothing physical has happened between you two?"

"Just a kiss. Some hand holding."

Joanna frowns. "You sure? You're not lying to protect him are you?"

Charlotte looks down at her bandaged hands as she speaks.

"I'm not. It was just a kiss. He is, was, my only friend." Charlotte glances up at Joanna. "That's why I am confused now. Why you are here? I didn't think *we* were friends."

Joanna sits back with a contemplative look on her face. "That's my bad. I tried making friends in the past, and all that got me was stabbed in the back, or used as a stepping stone on other people's way up. I am not the quirky best friend. I am the main character of my own life." She reaches for her tea and takes a long sip. "I'm not at Thornfield to make friends, I'm here to get a degree and make a career for myself. I swore off getting into other people's business years ago. But watching that man take advantage of you in your vulnerable moments, I am starting to feel like none of this would have happened if I had just been a little friendlier."

"He hasn't taken advantage of me."

Joanna gives her a look.

"Oh, the tenured professor didn't take advantage of the lonely graduate student in her twenties?"

"You make me sound pathetic."

Joanna sets down her cup and places a hand on Charlotte's arm.

"You are *not* pathetic. You were vulnerable and he took advantage of it. I am sorry I didn't do anything before, I should have. I sensed something was up, but I was too wrapped up in my own life. I wasn't a friend to you before. But I can start being one now, if you let me."

Charlotte is touched at the other girl's words.

"Really?"

"Really. But, I can't save you from all your bad decisions. You are going to have to start taking better care of yourself."

"How?"

"I can't really tell you that. You have to find out for yourself. I am here if you ever need advice. I do not dole out my advice lightly. If I give it and you ignore it, I am not going to give it again. You understand?"

"I understand. Thanks Joanna."

"You're welcome." Joanna responds gruffly. "Now, do you have a spare set of pjs for me?"

The two girls chat deep into the night. When sleep comes for Charlotte she isn't thinking of Dr. O' Farrell at all.

     

# CHAPTER TWENTY FOUR

## CURA

The winter break is over and classes soon begin once more. Charlotte returns to Thornfield to receive her new teaching assistant assignment. She is pleased to see that this semester, she and Joanna will be co-assistants for Cat's class.

On her way from the seminar room to her office, she pops her head into Cat's open door. The older woman is sitting at her desk, typing away at her computer. She looks up at Charlotte's knock, her blue light prescription lenses flashing cerulean against the glare of her screen.

"Come in!"

Charlotte steps into the office and takes a seat across from the professor's chair.

Cat's office is the polar opposite of Dr. O' Farrell's. Everything is well ordered. All the professor's books have their place on the bookshelves behind her, alphabetically of course. The window on the wall of her office has a set of retro floral curtains. Today Cat's hair is styled in a bouffant. She is wearing a corduroy pinafore dress, a peter pan collared blouse beneath it. Her make up is reminiscent of Twiggy, with blue eyeshadow and lower lashes drawn on with a pencil.

"How are you holding up?" Cat asks kindly, glancing at Charlotte's hands.

"Much better. I couldn't type for a while, but thank goodness for speech to text."

"Yes, it is amazing what technology can do. I am so glad to hear you are getting better."

"Thanks. I am glad to be working with you this semester."

"Oh yes! It will be lovely to have you and Joanna with me this semester. I think you'll find I have a different, ah, shall we say style of teaching than Ellis."

Charlotte feels the now familiar stab of pain at his name. Before she arrived that morning to the Art History department she dreaded running into him in the hallway. Yet when she saw his closed office door she felt a different sort of dread.

Carefully measuring the tone of her voice Charlotte says, "I didn't see him this morning. Is he not going to be at the orientation?"

Cat's brows rise in surprise. "Oh, didn't anyone mention? Ellis is taking a sabbatical this semester. I'm surprised he didn't tell you himself. I thought the two of you were getting along so well."

"I guess he forgot to mention it." Charlotte bites at her lip.

"Well, no need to worry! He's always available by email if you need him."

Charlotte doesn't think what she has to say to him should be conveyed over email but she is glad to hear he is not completely off the grid.

"On the topic of Ellis," Cat begins, her tone changing, "there is something I want to discuss with you."

Charlotte's heart begins to pound. Did she know? Did Joanna tell her?

"Ellis mentioned to me that you had been struggling with some anxiety last semester."

Charlotte feels instantly relieved. Cat didn't know. Then she feels a stab of betrayal. How could Dr. O' Farrell tell Cat about her private struggles?

Her feelings must have appeared on her face as Cat quickly added, "He didn't tell me exactly what brought it on, just that you were having a bit of a difficult time and that I should keep an eye on you. I would be remiss if I did not tell you that as part of your tuition at Thornfield there are all sorts of resources available to you through the student clinic. Counselling, or, if you need it, you can make an appointment to see one of the campus doctors."

"Why would I do that?"

Cat's mouth opens in an o of surprise. "Oh, well. If you need more than just counselling perhaps there is something a doctor could prescribe that may help as well?"

Charlotte frowns.

"I never thought of that. I never thought much of my mental health growing up. I was raised to think that it was selfish not to be grateful for what I had, that if something was wrong I was the problem, and I wasn't working hard enough to appreciate what was in front of me."

"Oh no, Charlotte. You are *not* the problem. There is nothing wrong with needing a little help. If it ever feels necessary, I urge you to make an appointment with the counsellor or the doctor if needed. I can even help you set up the appointment."

Warmth floods through Charlotte, touched by Cat's words. "Thank you Cat. I can make an appointment myself."

Cat nods. "Good. Good. Well, shall we discuss our class for the semester? I like to talk to my TAs before we start to see if they are comfortable with the course material first. If you are not, that is alright, we can arrange alternatives if necessary. I did think the class might spark some interest in you given your research focus. My class explores depictions of sexual violence in art. A heavy topic for sure, but one that *must* be discussed. Are you comfortable with that?"

Charlotte nods. If it was anyone else teaching the class she might have hesitated but knowing Cat she knows that the subject would be handled with all the care and knowledge it deserves.

"Oh good, I was hoping you would stay on! I feel like this course may give you some ideas on your own research on trauma and art."

The two spend some time talking about interdisciplinary approaches to the course and Charlotte leaves the meeting feeling excited about the semester ahead.

As she makes her way home she passes the University Centre and pauses, her earlier discussion with Cat about mental health rising to the surface. Though she is loathe to admit it, she does need help and the university offers the resources that she needs.

She steps through the door of the University Centre and heads towards the Student Health Centre.

Charlotte makes an appointment to see one of the campus doctors with mixed feelings. She does not want to admit she has a problem, but she cannot keep ignoring it any longer, she needs help.

Charlotte has struggled with anxiety her entire life. When she is anxious she will take seemingly normal situations and blow the smallest details out of proportion, convincing herself that everything is ruined. She calls it "snowballing," as if she is taking her small insecurities in her my palms and rolling them among all her other fears until they became one large mass of overwhelming dread. After reading about anxiety online Charlotte starts to make an effort to become aware when she begins to snowball and tries to redirect her thoughts. But after the incident with Geoff, and the pressures of graduate school mounting, Charlotte finally has to admit she needs to do more than just google her problems.

A week passes and it is time for her appointment. Her stomach is in knots. Soon her name is called and she follows the nurse into the examination room. Charlotte perches atop the examination table, her legs swinging, feeling like a child. The nurse asks her some questions and makes some notes on her chart. She stands and announces the doctor will be in soon and then leaves Charlotte with her thoughts.

To get the help she needs Charlotte must be honest, must tell the truth. But after pretending to be okay for so long, the truth is buried within her, she must search deep within herself until she comes away with that truth clutched in her hands, truths so close to her own heart her breath catches in her lungs as she thinks of speaking them aloud. Too many of the truths she finds within herself are too sharp, she fears that she will draw blood if she digs too deep.

When her father left her family all those years ago she believed it was her fault. That if she had been a better student, a better sister, a better daughter, her father might have stayed and their family would still be together. From that moment onwards Charlotte has strived to do better, to be better, to work so hard at being the best version of herself she could be to the people around her that she isn't even sure who *she* is any longer. Her life feels like a performance and she is finally beginning to tire of acting. And now, now she wants to find her true self, to show it to the world, she is afraid. Afraid of being rejected again for who she is, afraid that she wouldn't be seen.

All these years fear has been her constant companion. Fear of failure, fear of being found out. Every conversation, every assignment, every presentation is now a test, is now the deciding factor of her own worth. Maybe if she starts taking something for her anxiety, that fear will finally disappear.

When the doctor enters the examination room and asks Charlotte what she needs help with, Charlotte finally speaks her unspoken truth. The truth is one long exhale from a breath held in for far too long. Once that breath is let out she feels dizzy from suppressing it.

The doctor diagnoses her with anxiety and depression and prescribes her something called a SSRI—Selective Serotonin Reuptake Inhibitors. The SSRIs would help her brain produce more serotonin.

Charlotte feels each word like a physical blow, flinching away from the doctor as she speaks. The doctor notes her reaction.

"I know it is not easy to hear that you may have a problem. But we are here to help you, and I think this medication is the first step."

The doctor explains that the SSRIs are not a cure, but an aid. That if Charlotte really wants to help herself she needs to confront her suppressed feelings with a therapist as well, to redirect her negative thoughts with cognitive behavioural therapy. Charlotte agrees to speak to a therapist. She takes the prescription from the doctor and feels the warm bloom of hope in her chest.

# CHAPTER TWENTY FIVE

## REMEDIUM

The first week Charlotte is on her new medication she feels strangely hollow. For someone who spent her whole life keenly feeling every emotion, now nothing seems of great importance. She is neither sad, nor happy. She feels as if she is floating around, watching herself from afar.

It is late at night but she is lying in her bed wide awake, staring into the dark above her, she can see the light of her laptop burning in the corner of her eye. She turns to face the laptop, closes her eyes and lets the light burn red spots against her eyelids. The sight of Dr. O' Farrell's stricken face as she rushed from his home often greets her when she closes her eyes. Since taking the medication prescribed to her, she does not feel angry or sad at the sight, but still every time she closes her eyes Dr. O' Farrell's face pops into her mind and her stomach lurches.

But she did not have time to think about Dr. O' Farrell right now.

The semester passes by in a blur. Cat's class is engaging and stimulating and she greatly enjoys spending time with the professor and with her co-assistant Joanna. Their tentative friendship of the winter break has developed into what resembles a real one, the two girls meeting for coffee outside of classes to talk about their coursework, their research, their lives. Though she feels strangely disconnected the first week on her new medication, soon she begins to feel more like herself. Or, more accurately, a better version of herself that is able to look at the events of her life rationally rather than emotionally. A version of her life where her constant barrage of negative emotions and intrusive thoughts are finally quiet and she can get on with her studies, and actually succeed.

In fact, she has been doing so well that she has been called into Cat's office and given an offer she cannot refuse.

"Rome. Are you kidding?"

Cat smiles. "Not at all! I often spend the summer pursuing my research. This year my research is taking me to Rome. And I would like you and Joanna to come with me."

"Seriously?"

"Seriously!" Cat laughs. "You two have been a godsend to me. In the past students have been less than enthusiastic about the class but you two have really engaged with the students and I can see that the work is resonating with you."

"It is. I love the cross disciplinary approach."

"I thought you would. While we are in Rome we will be embracing the art historical side of things, getting to see the grand master's in their element. While it is all well and good to study a work of art from a textbook or a slide, it really isn't the same as seeing it in person. I understand that not everyone is privileged enough to fly to Europe and galavant around museums. So I would like to give you that chance."

"I appreciate that so much. Thank you, Cat."

"Thank you, Charlotte. You have been doing so well as my TA, and in your courses in general. You deserve this."

Charlotte leaves the meeting feeling euphoric. Once she accepts Cat's offer, for the first time since she started her medication, Charlotte feels the stirrings of emotion within her. Excitement flutters in her stomach.

Despite her initial excitement, Charlotte does not sleep well that night. She spends the long hours of the night tossing and turning, thinking of what may go wrong, what she might do to disappoint Cat and make her regret her decision to bring her along.

Darkness floods her room but Charlotte is still awake, biting at her lip and staring at the ceiling. Though her mind races with thoughts of disaster her body does not feel its usual effects of racing heart and panting breaths. She is distantly aware that she is scared. Scared of everything that awaits her, that too many good things have happened and something bad is lurking around the corner.

When the negative thoughts and emotions pile up, Charlotte redirects her thoughts. She thinks of something she can see, something she can hear, something she can feel, and something she can smell. She can see the headlights of cars as they pass along the road outside. She can hear the murmurs of her neighbour's television next door. She can feel her cool cotton sheets, and she can smell the laundry detergent she used to wash them.

She closes her eyes and sleep soon finds her. In her dreams she sees Rome.

     MEAGAN CLEVELAND

The remainder of the semester passes by in a blur. Charlotte marks essays and exams all while preparing for the trip to Rome in early June. The upcoming trip has only brought Charlotte and Joanna closer, the two texting about what they will do when they get there, what they will wear, what they will eat. It would be the first trip outside of the country for both of them.

Amidst the busy time, thoughts of Doctor O' Farrell still come to her every now and again. It is as if he has simply disappeared. Charlotte has not reached out to him, nor he to her. One day, curiosity getting the better of her, she makes the trip to his house, which sits empty and cold, the lights turned off, grass overgrown and weeds taking over the flower beds. He isn't at Thornfield, and he isn't at home, so where exactly is Dr. O' Farrell?

"Didn't you hear?" Adele says to her one day as they mark their respective exams in companionable silence. "Dr. O' Farrell's mother-in-law is sick. She was diagnosed with the same cancer her daughter had."

"That's terrible." Even though her first and only meeting with Mrs. Mason had been a sorry affair, she would not wish such a fate on even her.

"That's why he suddenly took his sabbatical. He's gone to stay with her while she is getting treatment."

"How kind of him." Charlotte replies, thinking of the box of journals in the basement. Did Mrs. Mason know what her son-in-law had done to her daughter?

"Wait," Charlotte spins in her chair to face Adele. "How did you know about that?"

"Bee told me." Adele shrugs.

Charlotte's eyes narrow at the mention of Adele's sister. "I thought he had a restraining order out on her?"

Adele's head whips up and she stares at Charlotte incredulously. "Is that what he told you? That's news to me."

"So, they are still in touch then?" Charlotte asks, her mind a flurry with memories of Blanche confronting Dr. O' Farrell the night of the snow storm, the stark outline of Blanche's shadow on Charlotte's bedroom wall as they fought for the journal.

"Not in touch no," says Adele carefully. "Truth be told, she is a little obsessed with him. She follows everything he does on his social media. I'm surprised you don't. I thought you two were close?"

"Not anymore."

Adele nods, hearing the finality in Charlotte's tone she drops the subject. The office is silent once more.

A few hours later Adele finishes her marking and takes her box of exam booklets out of the office, bidding Charlotte good night. Charlotte has yet to finish marking her stack of exams but, the moment Adele leaves the office she takes out her phone and searches Dr. O' Farrell's name. Though the professor does not have Facebook, Instagram, or even Linked In, she does discover a Twitter account in his name.

She scrolls through his account, seeing pictures of an old house with a garden brimming with tulips and daffodils, a short caption beneath titled "Spring", another of the same garden, roses trailing up the trellis captioned "Summer." She does not recognize the house but she deduces it must belong to Mrs. Mason. This must be where he is now staying.

She continues scrolling and pauses at a picture taken of Dr. O' Farrell at a past conference. It is a candid shot of him standing at a podium, his face alight with a smirk, no doubt after delivering one of his jokes. She goes to scroll past and her thumb hovers over the like button and a pink heart appears on the screen.

Oh no.

Charlotte hastily clicks the like button again and the heart disappears. But the damage is done. She drops her phone on the desk, watches it until the screen shuts off and turns black. She is about to turn to the small stack of exams on her desk but her phone lights up again. She glances at its screen, dread mounting. A notification. Charlotte has received a Twitter message from Dr. O' Farrell.

Minutes pass. Charlotte stares at the screen until it goes dark once more, not moving in her seat. Should she check the message? Should she finish marking, then check it? Should she finish marking, not check the message, and leave it unchecked for the rest of her life? She gnaws at her thumbnail as she thinks. As she hasn't moved in some time, the motion activated lights shut off and Charlotte sits in darkness. The screen of her phone lights up once more. This time with a text message. This one she cannot ignore, she has already seen the message before her phone darkens again.

**Charlotte, please.**

Two words. She is nearly undone by those two words alone. Even her medication cannot stop the sudden flow of emotion that overtakes her, a sadness that grips at her heart like a fist.

The phone lights up again, this time with a phone call.

She is frozen with indecision.

Should she pick up?

She listens to the phone, on silent, as it buzzes against the surface of her desk. The call ends but a message pops up on the screen. She cannot help herself, as she moves to pick up the phone and listen to the message the lights come back on.

"Charlotte. I know you're still angry with me but please, let me explain. I miss you Grey. I feel like a piece of me is missing, like you are a phantom limb. Not not a limb, my soul. My soul has been torn in two. Please bring back the other half. Please."

Charlotte does not delete the message. Instead she listens to it again. And again.

**Please.**

**Please.**

**Charlotte.**

Tears stream down her face and she presses the phone harder against her ear.

She cannot deny that she has felt the same way without him, as if a part of her is gone, torn in two, left only with an open wound slow to heal. That wound has reopened at the sound of his voice. But instead of tending to it she makes it worse, listening to his words over and over, the sound of her name on his lips like a prayer doomed to go unanswered.

How could she still feel this way after what he had done? What could he say that would excuse his actions?

The worst part is, she wants to call him back, wants to give him the chance to defend himself, to prove himself worthy of her love once more so they can go back to the way they were.

As she sobs the lights go off a second time.

# CHAPTER TWENTY SIX

## URBS AETERNA

Charlotte is now at the airport. There is no one at the departures gate to wave her goodbye but she does not mind. Part of this new chapter of her life is learning to enjoy her own company, to become the person she needs to be, to not have to rely on anyone else. A trip to another country on her own seems like a good place to start.

Charlotte gets in line to check her baggage looking over her shoulder anyway to glance at the families gathered at the gate, waving cheerfully at their loved ones in line. One day, one day she would have someone like that waving goodbye to her.

Once she is through security Charlotte strolls through the airport, stopping at the tiny coffee shop to get a latte. She immediately regrets her choice when she feels the first churning in her stomach and has to rush to the washroom to be sick.

It is Charlotte's first flight on an airplane. She keeps close to the washroom, darting in and out to dry heave above the questionably clean toilets. When her stomach, and her nerves, finally calms down she sits and waits.

Her phone buzzes. She glances down to see a text message from Geoff. Now out of the hospital and back at home, Geoff is doing much better.

**At the airport?**

Charlotte's thumbs fly across her screen as she replies.

**I'm through security, just waiting**

**for the flight to board.**

**You are so brave doing all this on your own. You're**

**going to have a great time! You've got this :)**

Bolstered by his words, Charlotte begins to feel a little lighter. She goes to sit at one of the little couches along the wall, taking out her charger to charge her phone while she waits. She wills her stomach to settle down, replaying what her brother wrote in her head.

*I am going to have a great time. I am going to have a great time.*

Soon, she even begins to believe it.

The acrobatics in her stomach start up again when they call for her flight to be boarded. Ticket and passport in hand, Charlotte lines up with the other travellers. There is a couple in front of her; a young man and woman. She watches the young man reach into his bag and pull out their tickets and passports, smiling at his partner, and Charlotte feels a sudden stab of loneliness. She has a vision of her and Dr. O' Farrell in line, his arm wrapped around hers, waiting to board their own flight together. The vision disappears as soon as it came, the memory of his betrayal still fresh in her mind.

She wouldn't be alone for long. Once she gets to Rome Cat and Joanna will be waiting for her.

After recovering from the initial terror of take off Charlotte begins to feel better about her flight. When her stomach begins to revolt against its contents once more she takes a motion sickness pill, not wanting to become too familiar with the air sickness bags. She sleeps for most of the flight.

She is wakes up when breakfast is carted out. She nibbles on a muffin and sips at some very weak coffee.

Finally, Charlotte arrives in Rome.

As she steps off the plane it suddenly hits her. She is very much on her own. In a foreign land. With very little knowledge of Italian.

As the surges of passengers jostle around her to catch their next flights or collect their bags, Charlotte stands stock still. She takes a deep breath and finds one of the airport staff in their neon jackets and asks where to get find her baggage. The older man kindly leads the way and Charlotte thanks him.

She watches the baggage carousel intently, fearing that her luggage would be lost, but sure enough there it is, her medium sized silver suitcase made more visible by the red ribbon she had tied to the handle the night before. Charlotte seizes her suitcase and rolls it out the doors.

There are crowds of people waiting outside. All around her people rush to friends and loved ones while Charlotte stands off to the side. In the back of the crowd she spots a sign bearing her name. Relieved, she approaches the sign attached to a giant, very sullen looking, man.

Cat arranged for a valet service to pick Charlotte up from the airport and take her to the apartment where she and Joanna would be staying. Charlotte smiles up at the valet. He curtly takes her suitcase from her and strides brusquely out into the sunshine. Charlotte rushes to keep up.

"I am glad to see you. I got so lost in the—"

*"Non parlo Inglese."*

Dampened by his curt reply Charlotte wordlessly follows him to a black car. He gestures for her to get in as he tosses her suitcase into the trunk. Although he does not speak any English, and she does not know much Italian, the drive is quite pleasant. The driver glances at Charlotte's t-shirt, which has an embroidered Eiffel Tower on the chest.

*"Tu parle français?"*

Charlotte brightens at the sound.

*"Oui!"*

Like most Canadian school children, Charlotte had taken French classes from elementary school until high school. She has some conversational skills and chatted with the driver. Soon her French is exhausted and the two lapse into silence.

Charlotte contents herself with gazing out of her window at the beautiful scenery. Terracotta and saffron buildings squat along the road, rooftop terraces spill with plants and bright pink flowers.

Soon they arrive at Charlotte's apartment on the *Via Amelia*, the building was the same terracotta orange as most of the others they passed along the way. The driver carries her bag up the stairs without a word while the building manager follows, chatting happily to Charlotte in English. The building manager lets her into her room and assures her that Joanna would be home within the hour.

While she waits she explores the apartment. The room is divided by a short wall that hides a king sized bed from view, the bed facing the bathroom door. A pull out couch rests against the short wall, the double bed would be for her,

Joanna had already claimed the king. Charlotte does not mind. She is happy to finally be there.

Soon Charlotte hears footsteps in the stairway. When the keys jingle in the door Charlotte jumps to her feet.

The door opens.

"You're here."

Joanna smiles broadly as she steps into the apartment. Joanna's typically cool demeanour has drastically changed. She is positively giddy.

"I'm here." Charlotte smiles.

"Together in Rome. Can you believe it?" She steps into the apartment, unloading her bag of groceries onto the table, chatting away as she moves.

"So do you want to come?" Joanna finishes.

Charlotte looks at her guiltily, she hasn't been listening. "Sorry, come where?"

"Come out for a walk around the city with me. I am going to the *Piazza Navona* to shop. I can show you the sights as we walk there."

"That would be great." Charlotte is thankful to get her first look at Rome without having to worry about getting lost on her own.

Joanna proves to be an excellent guide. Their apartment is minutes away from the Vatican and to get to the *Piazza Navona* the two pass through the *Piazza San Pietro,* otherwise known as St. Peter's square. They pass by many touristy gift shops along the way and Charlotte makes a mental note of ones to visit on her own. The two young women walk alongside the busy narrow road until they approach a wall of tall white marble columns, walking in between them and out into Saint Peter's square. The square is centred around Saint Peter's Basilica, a square white structure with a dome. Joanna explains how, during the afternoon, the basilica is crowded with lines of tourists waiting to get a look inside. Since it is now late afternoon there are only a few idling couples and a small group of nuns chatting beside the barricade. In the centre of the square is an Egyptian obelisk with a cross stuck on the top to make it less pagan. Joanna points to the rows of columns surrounding the square, statues carved by one of Charlotte's favourite artists, Bernini, sitting atop. Joanna explains that Bernini designed the square, and that each statue depicts a saint. The columns, running four rows deep, are dizzying to look at. Joanna guides Charlotte over to a small white circle amidst the grey stones on the ground. The words *centro del colonnato* are written inside the white ring.

"Stand right here," Joanna instructs, positioning Charlotte on the grey circle inside the white ring, her hands on Charlotte's waist. "Now look," she smiles when Charlotte gasps. The row upon row of white columns align from that very spot. "That's math for you," Joanna steps away, her hands dropping from Charlotte's waist as the two leave the square.

Joanna waves towards the entrance of the Vatican, guarded by men in outfits with stripes of blue, red and gold, with a high white collar, and matching puffy striped pants. A floppy black hat sits atop their heads, a pointy spear in their hands. There are even more gift shops beside charming *trattorias* with red and white striped awnings, couples and families dining at their outdoor tables. The girls keep walking until Charlotte spots what she knows to be Hadrian's Mausoleum, also known as the *Castel San Angelo,* a Roman emperor's tomb converted into a fortress in the Middle Ages. The fortress looms over the river, the ancient stone overseeing the crowds meandering along its banks. They walk across a bridge dotted with statues of angels to cross the Tiber into Rome proper.

While Charlotte is confident she can find her way around St Peter's square and the Vatican and not get too lost she is positively overwhelmed by all the twists and turns Joanna takes to get to the *Piazza.* All the gold and orange buildings look alike and Charlotte strives to keep Joanna in her sights.

Soon they arrive at *Piazza Navona*, a charming area with three large fountains, another obelisk, and scores of artists selling their works, along with street performers. As they enter the *Piazza* they pass a toy store, its walls painted the same pale orange as peach sorbet, and dotted with large windows. Each window displays different scenes: in one, gnomes and fairies sit amongst twisting greenery, in another, a large pegasus rears among cotton ball clouds and other mythical beasts suspended on wires in front of a blue backdrop. Charlotte longs to look inside but Joanna continues on her way so Charlotte quickly follows lest she lose the other girl. Joanna points at the fountains as they pass.

"More Bernini. He worked on these two fountains. That one is the *Fontana die Quattro Fiumi,* the Fountain of the Four Rivers. They would be," she begins to count them off with her fingers, "The Nile, the Danube, the Ganges, and, some river in America, honestly I can't remember all the details but we've got a book in the apartment you can read. That one there is the *Fontana del Moro,* the Fountain of the Moors. And that one is the *Fontana del Nettuno*, the Fountain of Neptune. Not Bernini this time, I'm afraid. Okay, now on to the Pantheon!"

She strides briskly on, Charlotte fights to keep up with her pace as fatigue from her flight threatens to overwhelm her. When they arrive at the Pantheon the sight takes Charlotte's breath away. It is stunning, even at night, the white marble bathed in golden street lights. She never really got a sense of how big it was until she stood beneath it, its columns so wide around it would take four people with their arms outstretched to surround them. Charlotte is admiring the Corinthian capitals when Joanna nudges her, pointing to the inscription beneath the pediment.

"*Marcus L F Agrippa Cos Tertium Fecit*. Marcus Agrippa, son of Lucius, that's the L F, *Lucii filius*, consul for the third time, made this."

"Latin. I'm impressed." Charlotte is, she tried to learn it but found it difficult.

Joanna grins. "Come on, let's go inside." The two girls cross the threshold and Charlotte is stunned by the sheer beauty of the place.

The interior is decorated with coloured marble in greens and orange. There are twelve niches along the circular room, serene statutes stand in each one.

"The Pantheon was converted into a Catholic Church in the Middle Ages, so all those statues are saints and whatnot. The most impressive thing, is up there." Joanna points above and they both look up. Charlotte knows that the Romans were innovative for their use of concrete and their ability to make domes. The coffered dome of the Pantheon is an impressive sight, even more so the *occulus*, or eye that opens the middle of the dome to the night sky. "The floor is tilted slightly to collect any rainwater that comes in through the *occulus*. In winter it will even snow through there."

After they have their fill of the marvels of the ancients, the two cross the square where the Pantheon sits, moving past the fountain and up the street to get gelato.

The gelato shop is heaven. Not only is the shop blessedly cool, it has a red awning outside, the interior covered with black and white tiles and a long silver counter that holds row upon row of colourful gelato. It is a veritable rainbow of frozen cream. Above the counter is a long chalkboard displaying the myriad of flavours. In Italian. Joanna laughs at Charlotte's baffled face, telling her to just point to the ones she wants. By chance, Charlotte chooses two complementary flavours, sour cherry and champagne. The two young women take their gelato outside, enjoying the rich flavours as they walk.

They wander the streets, passing the mausoleum of Augustus, the first emperor of Rome. The mausoleum is nothing like the fortress dedicated to Hadrian across the river, it definitely looks like a ruin, the golden stone crumbling and overrun with weeds. Across the road a sleek, modern concrete and glass building houses one of Augustus' most famed monuments; the *Ara Pacis*. Since it is so late it is closed, but Charlotte can see the white marble Altar of Peace through the glass. Charlotte feels she knows enough about the *Ara Pacis* from past Art History finals yet she has even more to learn from Joanna. Joanna is a veritable fount of knowledge,

           MEAGAN CLEVELAND

she even translates some of the Latin inscription along the side of the building, her gelato dripping down her arms as she neglects it. When Charlotte voices that she is impressed Joanna smiles.

"We read the *Res Gestae* in my Latin class so I've seen it before."

*"Res Gestae?"*

"Yeah, basically Augustus wrote down all the things he did."

They take what Joanna calls 'the scenic route' back, pointing out historical monuments and sights of interest as they go. As they navigate the bustling Italian roads, Joanna even attempts to teach Charlotte some Italian, however, the verb conjugations go right over her head.

Nestled amidst the busy roads and the modern buildings lining the street is another Roman ruin, rising from beneath the busy sidewalks are crumbling columns along a long gone rotunda. Not only is the site submerged below street level, it is marked off by a black fence. Charlotte pauses and goes up to lean against the fence, looking down at the ruins.

"That is the *Largo Argentina*. Historically it's known for housing the remains of Pompey's theatre. The general and triumvir Pompey, not to be confused with the place Pompeii," Joanna explains as she joins Charlotte at the fence. "Now its known for something different." She pauses, deliberately waiting for Charlotte to ask.

"What is it known for now?"

"Just look." She answers, a tad dramatically. Charlotte looks down to see flashes of colour dart among the grass.

"Are those—"

"Cats." Joanna responds. Sure enough, now that Charlotte knows what to look for, she can see scores of feral cats roaming the ruins, some stalking pigeons through the grass, others reclining on the ruins themselves, seeping in the day's warmth from the stone.

"That's amazing."

"The city is pretty amazing."

The two stop at one of the colourful *trattoria* on their way back, filling up on pasta and wine. Once they are filled to the brim they make their way back to their apartment. Charlotte is so tired she falls asleep almost as soon as her head touches the pillow. She does not need to remind herself to have a good time.

# CHAPTER TWENTY SEVEN

## VIDERE

Charlotte decides the next morning to venture out on her own. She has no trouble finding her way to St. Peter's Basilica. That morning she dresses modestly for her trip, choosing a green gingham dress with sleeves that cover her shoulders and a hem that hangs below her knees, and a straw hat to keep off the sun.

It is so early in the morning, there is virtually no line to get inside the church. The church is utterly beautiful. It has that unique smell that only churches have, of old wood, dust and incense and the sweat of too many people crammed in too small a space. Her Catholic upbringing has Charlotte crossing herself as she enters, dipping her fingertips in the warm holy water and touching her fingers to her forehead, shoulders and chest. She looks around the church itself for about half an hour, marvelling at Michelangelo's *Pieta*, at the intricate marble walls and floor and the golden script that runs below the ceilings.

She steps outside to the glaring light of the sun. Charlotte closes her eyes against the glare, savouring the feeling of warmth that bathes her face. With a smile she makes her way to the Vatican City.

While she waits in line to enter the Vatican, Charlotte practises Italian over and over in her head until it is her turn, stammering *"Uno bigletto per favore,"* the man at the desk hands her a ticket with a wink.

Charlotte spends a long time looking at Christian art, seeing a few works by artists she studied in school. After descending the steep spiral staircase she had seen so many pictures of online, she makes the long trek to the Sistine Chapel through a series of long halls all studded with statues, paintings and hoards of tourists taking pictures of *everything*. When she steps into the Sistine Chapel a hush descends. Charlotte is awestruck by the writhing figures all along the walls peering down at her from the ceiling painted all those years ago by Michelangelo. Charlotte marvels at the sense of movement of the figures, the richness of the paint, and the sheer scope of the work. Charlotte is convinced there is nothing more impressive than the Sistene Chapel, only to come face to face with Raphael's *School of Athens* right as she is leaving, lingering to mentally identify the figures in the painting.

Charlotte finally stumbles outside into the mid-afternoon sun, in a daze, and tries to find somewhere to eat lunch. She stops at one of the *trattoria* that dot the road, sitting at a table with a red and white checkered tablecloth. A waiter appears out of nowhere and proffers her sparking water, which she does not much like the taste of but drinks anyways to stay hydrated. She dines on paper thin slices of prosciutto with balls of mozzarella.

Charlotte finds her way back to St.Peter's with little trouble but is disorientated when she passes through the large white pillars of St. Peter's Square. She cannot remember how to get back. Charlotte feels the first effects of a panic attack, a heavy weight on her chest, her breath coming rapidly.

Spinning on the spot, she recognizes the colourful awning of a particular shop and realizes where she is.

She can do this.

When she steps back into the apartment Joanna is up and dressed, reading an article on her laptop at the kitchen table.

"Cat wants us to meet her at her place for dinner tonight."

"That sounds nice." Charlotte replies as she eases into the chair across from Joanna.

"We should grab a bottle of wine on the way there."

"Great idea."

Charlotte recounts her morning adventures until it is time to depart.

Cat's apartment is in the heart of the city. Charlotte expects it to be a modern apartment like theirs and is surprised by Cat's penthouse in an old building with antique furniture, dark wood trim and walls painted with cherubs. Charlotte perches on the antique sofa while Joanna offers a delighted Cat the bottle of wine they bought on the way over. Cat is in her element, dressed as Audrey Hepburn in Roman Holiday in a circle skirt, blouse and silk neck tie. Her bright orange hair pulled back in a ponytail.

"Thank you girls, this is lovely." Cat smiles as she pours a glass for each of them. Charlotte holds the glass without taking a sip while Cat disappears to bustle about her kitchen. She soon reappears with a charcuterie board piled with a spread of cured meats and cheeses, olives, pesto, and dried fruit. The three women enjoy their food, sip their wine, and talk about the city.

"Tell me all your adventures so far."

Charlotte and Joanna recount their walk around the city. Joanna arrived a few days earlier and explored many of the museums on her own. Charlotte listens to her intently, noting the change in the other girl's demeanour. At Thornfield, Joanna is very closed off, almost distant, to the others in the department. When the two of them go out together for coffee or study together in Charlotte's apartment, Charlotte could see Joanna's playful side. But here, in Rome, it is as if a weight has been lifted from her shoulders. Joanna's carefully neutral expression is gone, a bright smile is fixed on her face. Charlotte wonders if the others can see a difference in herself as well.

Having finished their wine, Cat gathers their glasses together and disappears into the kitchen again. When she comes back out she has three new glasses and another bottle. She passes them to the two young women and asks them to take it upstairs while she gets dinner.

Charlotte sets the glasses and bottle on a tray while Joanna takes a stack of plates and lays cutlery on top. The two ascend a narrow staircase, push open the door at the top and find themselves on a private rooftop terrace. A startled laugh bubbles from Charlotte's lips, she is enchanted by the rooftop garden spilling with colourful flowers and greenery, a string of lights twinkling in the twilight. The two set the table and soon Cat emerges with plates of arancini and pizza balanced precariously on top a bowl of salad.

"I am so glad to have the two of you here, it is far nicer than drinking alone."

"Now that we are all together, what is the plan?" Charlotte asks.

"Plan?" Cat repeats after taking a sip of wine.

"The plan for your research? What do you need us to do?"

"Oh, that." Cat drains the rest of her glass and sets it down on the table with a soft clink. "That's all handled. You two are free to enjoy yourselves."

"But, aren't we going to help you with your research?" Charlotte frowns.

"I did what I needed to do this morning. I had a meeting with the museum curators and they let me view a painting for my next article. On paper you two are helping me with my research, but in reality, this is really a chance for you to explore the city and find inspiration for your writing. All I need for you to do is to experience all the city has to offer. Go, look at art, taste food, and come back next semester with a new appreciation for your studies."

Charlotte is stunned. She came on this trip to work, to learn from Cat, only to find she is on a glorified vacation. Cat spots the look on her face and reaches across the table to grasp Charlotte's hand.

"I know what you are thinking. But this is not it. You are not here to *just* sight see. I want you to seek out works of art you have long admired, to study them in person. You can write down your opinions if you like, though it is not necessary. Like I said before we came here, it isn't enough to simply look at reproductions in a textbook. You need to *see* the canvas, to discover the layers of paint, the way they are displayed, the information the museum or gallery chooses to share about the work and how it differs or compares to what you already know. You are here to learn. But not from me. From Rome itself."

Charlotte is glad of Cat's kindness and grateful to have been brought along. But she feels slightly guilty there is nothing to show for her time here, no articles for her to work on, or papers to write. The thought of just experiencing art in person is a dizzying one, one that is almost overwhelming. A few months ago she escaped her abusive home, her small town she feared she would be trapped in forever. Now she is on an all expenses paid (or more specifically, paid and then reimbursed by the department) trip, and she isn't expected to earn it? It almost feels too good to be true, that Charlotte should be steeling herself, waiting for the other shoe to drop. To hear that all Cat wants is for her to learn and enjoy herself is beyond comprehension.

She feels as if she does not deserve it.

     MEAGAN CLEVELAND

# CHAPTER TWENTY EIGHT

## ARTEM

Charlotte and Joanna visit the Villa Borghese together the next day. It is a bit difficult figuring out the busses but they manage to find the right bus, luckily the bus stop is right outside their door. They take the bus across the city, and transfer to another, smaller bus that speeds through alleyways, wincing as it careens through the narrow spaces between the terracotta coloured buildings.

The gallery itself is situated in the middle of a lush green park. Tall trees shade the two young women from the hot Italian sun. It is still fairly early in the morning, the weather is cool, a nice change from their scorching forays in the afternoons.

The Borghese Gallery is as beautiful as the Vatican, the building itself is just as much a work of art as the paintings, statues and busts that adorn its walls. The walls are made of different types of marble, white, and red threaded with purple veins, with mouldings gilt in gold. The ceilings of each room are painted with different scenes, some rooms replicate the Pompeian styles of wall painting, other depict leering satyrs gazing down, with scenes of revelry taking place directly above. Bronze busts of Roman emperors sit throughout the gallery. Charlotte is impressed by the sheer number of paintings, in particular the Renaissance masters, loving the stark contrast of the Caravaggios, and the bright colours of Raphael. The paintings are wonderful.

But it is the marble masterpieces by Bernini that take her breath away. *Apollo and Daphne. The Rape of Proserpina.* Both works depicts the gods trying to take off with the objects of their desires, the former failed while the latter succeeded, taking his prize to be his wife in the underworld. Pluto's face is stern, his diadem of invisibility sitting atop his curls. Proserpina fights against him, writhing away from his touch, her arm braced against his face. Charlotte's high school art teacher always said it was not enough to view a statue head on, but to experience it in the round. Charlotte circles around the statue, horrified by the casual violence depicted there, the way Pluto's fingers seem to dig into the soft flesh of Proserpina's thighs. Pluto grimaces as he struggles to subdue Proserpina, her own face frozen in a look of anguish. Cerberus, the three headed dog who guards the entrance of the Underworld, stands watch beside them.

*Apollo and Daphne* is also awe-inspiring. Apollo lacks the stern gravitas of his divine uncle, he is all youth and beauty. Bernini captures the moment in which Daphne, the object of Apollo's desire, turns into a laurel tree to escape him. Daphne is forever trapped in a moment of transformation: the tips of her hair, her fingers, her toes, become twisting branches, leaves creep up her legs, her face frozen. But is her face frozen in a moment of wonder or a moment of terror at her transformation? Blinded by his

      MEAGAN CLEVELAND

desire, Apollo is oblivious, a smile playing at his lips as he reaches for his prize.

Charlotte marvels at the statues. Each depicting an infamous rape of mythology. Artemisia Gentileschi, a Baroque painter and rape victim herself, was criticized for her painting of *Susanna and the Elders* for depicting a moment of such violence and was forced to repaint her subject in a more temperate, feminine style. Whereas Bernini, a man, could depict moments of violence to great acclaim, his work taking pride of place, moments of extreme violence preserved in marble for all to see.

While Charlotte admires Bernini's skill at capturing movement and facial expressions in marble she cannot help but be unnerved by the subject matter. In the past she had been an avid admirer of Bernini's, however, after spending the last several months assisting Cat to teach her course on depictions of sexual violence in art, she finds herself perturbed by this particular collection of pieces. Charlotte does not know whether to be horrified at Proserpina and Daphne's expressions of horror, their unending sentence of forever reliving the moment of their greatest terror, or should she begrudgingly respect that Bernini chose to depict the women's reactions to the act of violence, acknowledging the severity of the situation. Should she feel a voyeur to the men's act of fulfilment, or is she bearing witness to the trauma suffered by the young women?

These questions plague her throughout the rest of her visit, her eyes now attuned to other works alluding to acts of violence: Diana and Actaeon, the rape of Danaë, David and Goliath.

What is humanity's enduring obsession with violence, the act itself and the prelude to it? Are the artists reliving their own worst moments, or forced to turn to imagination, never having experienced it themselves?

Charlotte and Joanna spend half the day at the gallery, inspecting every sculpture, every painting, and even the walls of the galleries themselves. Charlotte's mind is abuzz with all that she has seen and she longs to quiet her racing thoughts.

Charlotte is grateful for the moment she steps out of the chilled marble halls and into the warm sunshine. She listens to the wind whisper through the trees, she feels the warm touch of the afternoon sun on her upturned face.

She is sitting cross legged on the grass while Joanna gets gelato. Joanna returns and hands Charlotte a cone. Charlotte finds herself staring at the cone while the frozen cream drips down her wrist.

"You're dripping." Joanna observes.

Charlotte snaps out of her reverie and mops up the mess with a napkin.

"Do you not like the flavour?" Joanna asks, her own cone devoured.

"Sorry, I was distracted." Charlotte offers the other girl a smile and digs in.

The two take their time returning to their apartment, lingering at shops and perusing their wares. On a long table filled with rows of replicas in white plaster, Charlotte purchases a small statue of Apollo and Daphne to remember her time at the gallery. The vendor wraps the statue in tissue and hands it over to Charlotte, who carefully places it within her bag.

She feels the weight of Daphne's suffering on her shoulders all the way home.

Charlotte wakes the next morning to a blood curdling scream. She jolts upright in her bed, to see Joanna hunched over the sink, screaming, a knife laying on the counter beside her. Joanna is clutching at her bleeding hand, tears welling in her eyes.

Charlotte rises from the bed and rushes over to the sink. "Let me see," She orders. Joanna turns to her questioningly and Charlotte adds "My mom's a nurse."

"I was trying to open the coffee packets, but there are no scissors so I—"

"Hacked at it with a knife?" Charlotte finishes.

Joanna grimaces. "Smart, I know."

Charlotte turns on the tap, running the water until it is warm then thrusts Joanna's hand under the flow. Joanna cries out as the water runs pink, washing the blood away to find the source: a jagged cut on her finger. Charlotte turns the water off and gently pats Joanna's hand dry with a towel. Charlotte strides to the bathroom down the hall and pulls off a length of toilet paper. She wraps the paper around Joanna's finger, the paper already growing red with blood. "Press tightly on the cut and hold your arm above your head, that'll make the blood flow more slowly."

"Do you think I should go to the hospital?" Joanna asks.

"I'm not sure." Charlotte looks around. The apartment is dark, it is only five am in the morning. "What if we go to the pharmacy around the corner? We'll ask the pharmacist if he thinks you need stitches and while we are there we can get you some bandages."

"We? Wouldn't you rather be out sightseeing and making the most of your day?" Joanna asks incredulously.

"Would you rather go alone?"

"No. I want you to come with me."

The two linger at the apartment for a few hours, waiting for the shops to open. Joanna watches Charlotte from where she sits on the bed, arm raised over her head to stop the blood flow to her finger.

"You know, it's probably safe for you to put your arm down now."

"It hurts." Joanna says quietly.

"Once the pharmacy opens we'll go over there and ask the pharmacist whether they think you should go to the hospital and have it looked at."

Charlotte draws out her phone and opens her email. She is biting at her thumbnail when Joanna interrupts her thoughts.

"What are you doing?"

Charlotte stands and goes over to the bed, sits next to the other girl and shows her the screen of her phone. The Thornfield Art History department sent out an email about a scholarship for a student at the graduate level. Charlotte is intrigued by the writing prompt: what is the purpose of art?

"Are you going to enter?" Joanna asks.

"I don't know." Charlotte bites her nails as she glances down at the screen.

"Adele told me you did a great presentation in your class. You're a good student, a good writer. What's the problem?"

"What if I don't get it?"

Joanna stares at her a moment. "Well, you won't know unless you enter."

Charlotte sighs. "True."

Joanna smiles. She rises from the bed, goes over to her open suitcase on the floor and pulls out her laptop with her good hand. She snaps it open and begins to type one handed. Once she has logged in she wordlessly hands the laptop over to Charlotte, the scholarship entry page open and waiting.

"You want me to do it now?"

"No time like the present." She squints at the clock on the wall. "We have another hour before the pharmacy opens. Get writing."

Charlotte takes the laptop and wanders over to the small kitchen table. She fills out the contact information of the form and then moves on to the essay portion. The cursor blinks as she stares at the screen.

Then she begins to write.

Charlotte writes about what she knows to be be true about art: throughout history art was a powerful medium to be commissioned by the elite to communicate their power. Though art may be commissioned by a king, the church, or a powerful merchant family, the artist conveys their own message in their art through their technical skill along with their own personal experiences. While a person can look at a work of art knowing all these facts, a work of art can also illicit an emotion or experience contrary to the message of the commissioner, or even the artist themselves. All throughout her academic career Charlotte has heard the words: art is subjective. Art can mean something different to each and every viewer. While knowledge of the artist and the time period it was created in can enrich the viewer's experience of a work of art, to Charlotte the prevailing power of art is the emotion it evokes. Earlier that day Charlotte tried, in vain, to examine the technical skill of Bernini, to admire the power of his patron Cardinal Scipione Borghese, but in the moment she first saw his sculptures in person, she was struck by the emotion the works evoked. The violence of Pluto's grasping hands, the anguish of Proserpina's face, the horror of Daphne's transformation. Viewing the work brought to mind Charlotte's own experience with violence, her brother's scarred wrists, her mother's pursed lips and clenched fists. Had Bernini suffered through his own traumas in order to communicate it through his art? Or was Charlotte's own experience's colouring her opinion of it? Did it even matter?

The words flow through Charlotte, a mixture of her knowledge of her subject and her own personal experiences. Though at the back of her mind she fears that someone, somewhere, will read her work and scoff, deep down she knows that it does not matter, that the importance of art is the experience of the viewer. That the importance of art mirrors the importance of the individual, whoever they may be.

Soon the morning sun streams through the window, warming the small apartment. Charlotte looks up to find it is well past the hour that Joanna set for her. She quickly rereads her work and hits send and shuts the laptop with a decisive snap.

Joanna looks up.

"Time to go?"

 MEAGAN CLEVELAND

The two make their way to the pharmacy and tell the pharmacist what happened to Joanna's finger. To get a look at it, the pharmacist promptly tears off the makeshift bandage and the cut begins to bleed again. Joanna's eyes well with tears and the pharmacist hurriedly puts the bandage back in place and goes to get them gauze and some antiseptic. He gives them instructions on how to clean the wound, assuring them that Joanna does not need to go to the hospital for stitches.

Relieved, the two walk around the corner back to the apartment. Charlotte helps to wash the cut in warm water and towels it dry. Once dry she puts on the antiseptic cream and wraps the wound with gauze.

"If this Art History thing doesn't work out for you, you could be a nurse." Joanna observes drily.

Charlotte laughs.

After Joanna is all bandaged up, she draws her wounded hand protectively against her chest. They are sitting together on the edge of Charlotte's pull out bed, the mattress dipped beneath their shared weight, drawing the two of them closer.

They sit there for a few minutes, neither of them speaking. The noisy hum of the refrigerator the only sound in the room.

Eventually, Joanna looks up at Charlotte through her lashes.

"I've had a really good time here with you."

Charlotte turns to face her with a smile. "Me too—" She begins but her words are cut off by Joanna's lips covering her own.

Joanna's lips are soft, her skin smells like her lavender soap. Charlotte leans into the kiss, overwhelmed by the touch of another person. Her eyes flutter closed. But in her mind's eye it is not Joanna sitting with her on the bed, her soft hands wrapped in her hair. No, it is another figure, his lips chapped, his hands calloused, but his touch gentle.

Charlotte's eyes snap open and she draws back.

"I'm sorry. I really like you Joanna, but I don't have feelings for you, not like that."

"I like you, you like me. It doesn't have to mean anything."

"It does to me."

Joanna nods in understanding. "I get it."

She shuffles away from Charlotte, putting some space between them.

"So, can I read your application?"

Glad of the change in subject, Charlotte shakes her head.

"Don't be like that, I'm sure it's fine."

"No," Charlotte laughs. "You can't read it because I already sent it."

Joanna raises her brows in surprise. "You sent it already? Sounds like you are confident with what you wrote."

"You know what? I am."

"Good. You should be. You know what you are doing. Watching you this week I've caught a glimpse of the kind of scholar you will become and I think this scholarship is the right step to set you on that path."

"Thanks, Joanna."

"Now, hand me my laptop. I am going to send in my own application." She holds out her good hand and Charlotte smiles as she crosses the room to the table. Joanna opens the laptop and begins to type one handed. She does not smile back, her attention focused on the screen.

  MEAGAN CLEVELAND

"While I work on this, I want you to go out and make the most of your last day here. Got it?" She looks up, her brown eyes boring into Charlotte's own.

"Got it."

Joanna smiles.

# CHAPTER TWENTY NINE

## SOLUS

Charlotte explores the city on her own, venturing past the familiar safety of St. Peter's Square and Hadrian's Mausoleum to cross the angel studded bridge.

Charlotte begins the *long* walk to the Roman Forum. Even though it is still early in the morning the sun is blazing and Charlotte can feel the heat settle on her skin like a heavy blanket. Thankfully her straw hat shields her from the sun's rays. Charlotte walks along the road in front of the Vittorio Emanuele monument, or as Cat calls it 'The Wedding Cake', and once she has walked past the large white building she gets her first sight of Ancient Rome.

The Forum is amazing, the ruins of the past peacefully laying amongst the grass, cornflowers sprout at the base of columns and white butterflies flutter past. Charlotte walks all around the Forum past the death site of Julius Caesar, where she picks some of the blue cornflowers dotting the site and tosses them onto the spot. She sees the remains of the Temple of Vesta, the Basilica Aemelia and the Basilica Iulia. The area is huge so she pauses at a shady spot at the bottom of the Capitoline hill to rest for a moment. After a drink and a reapplication of sunscreen Charlotte continues. She passes the Forum of Vespasian to the Palatine hill to see the Domus Augustus. She is surprised to see the hill is covered with orange trees and watches other tourists take off their shoes to throw them up at the trees, hoping to get an orange.

After exploring what seems to be every inch of the Forum, Charlotte crosses the road to a restaurant across from the Colosseum to enjoy a Caprese salad: buffalo mozzarella, tomato slices and basil leaves drizzled with balsamic vinegar and olive oil. Even though she made sure to drink throughout the day, the blazing sun gives her a pounding headache and Charlotte is desperate for some caffeine. She is a little dismayed to see the tiny cup of espresso placed before her, which she promptly finishes in one large gulp, wishing for the super sized drinks of North America. Even though the cup is tiny Charlotte finds her pounding headache is soon cured, the diminutive cup of espresso giving her the energy needed for the Colosseum.

Charlotte is most excited for the Colosseum. One of her good memories of her mother was the charm bracelet she received for her thirteenth birthday. Charlotte credits the small charm of the Colosseum with the beginnings of her fascination with art, architecture and history. Though her mother did not approve of her studies, she had inadvertently set her on the path to where she is today. Since she bought her ticket at the Forum, Charlotte did not have to wait in the long winding line at the entrance, instead walking right in. Walking along the first floor of the Colosseum, looking at the remains of the stone seating and the stage where the gladiators would fight, now gone, and the maze like structure beneath that the gladiators and the beasts they fought would use to ascend to the stage. She then went up the steep stairs to see the temporary exhibit on display. The temporary display about ancient libraries is utterly fascinating, Charlotte is glad for the reprieve from the sun as she looks at the display. After leaving the amphitheatre, she walks outside along the Forum of Trajan to view Trajan's column, a tall pillar of marble with the emperor's Dacian campaign incised in the stone in panels reminiscent of an unwound film reel.

Charlotte soon stops to sit, enjoying her independence. She is proud of herself for going out this far into the city on her own, proud of taking a chance and submitting that application. She knows that she can handle whatever is ahead of her at Thornfield. Not only her classes, her anxiety, her fraught relationship with her family, Charlotte has found the courage she needs to face her fears and be the person she knows she can be.

As proud as she is of her independence she can't help but wish she could share this feeling with someone. The someone on her mind is the last person she should be thinking of.

The next morning Charlotte pulls along her luggage and boards a bus to Termini Station to head to the airport by train.

Charlotte had been driven from the airport to the apartment when she arrived in Rome, she worries she will get lost on her way back to the airport. Termini Station bustles with crowds of people, the lights bright, the voices loud. Charlotte is surprised to find that she is not panicking. She calmly waits for her train to arrive.

     MEAGAN CLEVELAND

When the sign flashes that her train is ready to depart Charlotte follows the crowds out the doors and onto the tracks and boards the train.

Charlotte puts her earbuds in her ears and spends most of the ride looking out the window, watching the scenery roll by while the carriage full of people rattles along. When the train comes to a jarring halt she feels the nerves begin to stir in her belly.

She steps off the train and into the airport. Though she fears the plane may be delayed, or she may miss it entirely due to the crowds of people queuing to go through security, Charlotte prints out her boarding pass, hands over her luggage and goes through the security gate without issue. She enjoys her last espresso in Italy and soon it is time to board the plane.

She finds her seat by the window and settles down for the long flight. She spent so much of the night before packing and then worrying about finding her way to the airport that she did not get much sleep that night. Her worries now behind her, tiredness catches up with her. Her paperback lies unopened on her lap and her eyes flutter closed.

Soon she begins to dream.

Charlotte is back at Thornfield, its stone walls obscured by shrouds of mist. Charlotte struggles to find her way, her feet catching at cracks in the sidewalk, at tree roots, or park benches. She feels as if she is fighting her way through a cloud, the great white expanse blinding her. As she struggles to find her way to Thornfield she hears a voice carried on the wind.

"Charlotte."

She pauses. The voice is familiar, the sound an invisible string tugging at her heart.

"Charlotte."

She turns on the spot, but she cannot see through the mist.

"Charlotte!"

"Ellis?" Charlotte begins to run, not caring that she cannot see, she feels that invisible string tighten around her heart the closer she comes to him, using the bind between them to find her way back to him.

That invisible string goes taut, its grip around her heart stealing her breath. And then, it snaps.

She feels the string slacken and dread fills her.

"Ellis!"

The mist clears and Charlotte finds herself in his office.

It is empty.

Charlotte jerks awake as an announcement fills the cabin. She remembers where she is, on a plane, in the sky, on her way home.

She counts the minutes until she can land.

She has to find Dr. O' Farrell.

# CHAPTER THIRTY

## QUAERERE

When the plane lands Charlotte rushes to grab her luggage from the baggage claim and make her way home.

She takes a taxi to her apartment, unlocks her door, rolls her unopened suitcase inside, then turns and locks the door again, already on her way to Thornfield.

The campus shines in the afternoon sun, the barren trees of winter now lush with green leaves, the campus gardens full of flowers. Charlotte hurries to the Art History department and rushes down the empty hall, her shoes clacking against the floor as she runs. Finally she reaches Dr. O' Farrell's office. She reaches for the door, but it is locked. She tries to peer through the glass but cannot see within, she cannot tell if the office is as empty as it was in her dream. As she stands there, her heart racing, her hair plastered to her forehead and the back of her neck, sweat staining her shirt, she thinks of how she must look. She turns and slowly makes her way to the bathroom where she splashes cold water on her face, willing her heartbeat to slow down. Calmer now, she heads back out into the hallway but does not return to Dr. O' Farrell's office. Instead she heads to her own office.

She is not surprised to see Adele at her desk, head phones in her ears, her eyes focused on the screen in front of her. Catching movement out of the corner of her eye she turns and spots Charlotte. She takes one of the earbuds out of her ear.

"Back from Rome?" She asks politely. Her tone is cool. Adele made no efforts to hide her jealousy once she heard of Charlotte and Joanna's trip.

"It was great." Charlotte replies.

Adele frowns.

"If it was so great why do you look like such a wreck? No offence." She adds, raising her hands in mock self defence.

"I just got off the plane."

"And you came straight here? Don't you need a break?"

Charlotte shakes her head, she can feel her pulse quicken with worry once more. Adele spots the first signs of a panic attack and stands from her desk and heads over to Charlotte and places a comforting hand on her arm.

"Let's go outside. Get some fresh air."

The two sit beneath the shade of an oak tree as Charlotte takes a deep breath in and out. She has been on her medication for some time now and is starting to find that it is not as effective as it once was. She has not felt the stirrings of a panic attack in some time, not since the dream.

"So why did you really come?" Adele asks, her jealousy over Charlotte's trip forgotten.

"This is going to sound so stupid," Charlotte begins, "but I had a dream about Dr. O' Farrell. He was in trouble."

Adele gapes at her.

"I knew it sounded stupid." Charlotte groans.

     MEAGAN CLEVELAND

"No, not stupid at all. How long has it been since you checked your campus email?"

Charlotte considers. She had not checked since the day Joanna kissed her, the day she saw the scholarship application and submitted her essay.

"A few days."

Adele's eyes widen.

"So you don't know?"

Charlotte frowns. "Know what?"

Adele's comforting pats on Charlotte's back suddenly cease. The other girl takes her own deep breath before she begins to speak.

"A few days ago the department sent out an email. Dr. O' Farrell went to pick up some things from his house. After packing up some fresh clothes he stopped to light a cigarette. You know how he smokes when he is stressed. And, well. He had been staying with his mother-in-law for so long, he didn't know about the gas leak."

"Gas leak?" Charlotte repeats, going cold with dread.

Adele nods. "There was a gas leak. The moment he lit his cigarette the house went up in flames. Parts of it collapsed. Thank god he was outside when it happened so he wasn't burned too badly, but he was hurt when the house fell down. They found him in the wreckage. He's been in the hospital ever since. They sent out an email to the whole department, I'm surprised you didn't see it when you were in Rome."

Though it is a warm summer's day, Charlotte feels as if she is encased in ice. She begins to shake as she thinks of herself having fun in Italy as Ellis, Dr. O' Farrell, was trapped under the rubble of his burning home.

"Is he okay?"

"I don't know."

"You didn't go to see him?" Charlotte asks incredulously.

"No, not after everything with him and Blanche." Adele says darkly.

"What did he do to Blanche?" Charlotte thinks of her last meeting with the woman, the accusations she made. Had Dr. O' Farrell stolen her work too?

"Remember what you said to me in the office a month ago? About a restraining order? You were right. He *did* get a restraining order. I thought she was a little obsessed with him but she was outright stalking him, breaking into his house even. Blanche has a criminal record now."

"And you're mad at him about that?"

"Not at him. At her. For lying and playing the victim this whole time. Turns out he was the victim." Lowering her voice, she leans closer to Charlotte to add, "When I heard about the fire I thought, you know, that Blanche had done something."

"Did she?"

Adele shakes her head. "No. She was at home with our parents when it happened. How messed up is it that my first instinct is to think she did it? That's why I didn't go to see him. I don't think he needs to be reminded of my sister on top of everything else he has to deal with right now. What about you? Are you going to visit him?"

"I don't know."

      **MEAGAN CLEVELAND**

Charlotte takes another taxi to Dr. O' Farrell's house. Or, what used to be his house. While most of the Georgian home is blackened albeit still standing, a portion of it had collapsed in on itself, that must have been where Dr. O' Farrell was buried. Charlotte shudders at the thought.

She walks up the long driveway and to the front of the house.

Charlotte steps through the doorway.

The home she had once compared to a fairytale is no longer the light and airy home of an enchanted princess. It is a ruin, the last remnants of an old kingdom reduced to ash. The once pale blue walls are blackened by smoke, the dark stain creeping up the walls to the high ceilings. A coat of ash covers the hardwood floors and carpet like a grey shroud. Charlotte walks through the empty house with only her memories for company. Memories of a whistling kettle, of pots of tea carried to the living room, of Trivial Pursuit laid out on the floor. Memories of an embrace in the upstairs hallway, of a kiss shared by the golden glow of the Christmas tree, of a voice calling her name through the snow. Memories of a figure in the dark, of a journal hidden in a pocket, memories of her world falling apart around her as she read its pages.

The basement door is ajar and Charlotte pushes it open, looking down the darkened staircase. She pulls out her phone from her pocket and shines its light down the stairs and makes her way down. The box of journals sits in the centre of the room, untouched. She approaches it cautiously, nudges the lid from the top and reaches inside. She pulls out journal after journal, all that remains of the late Antoinette O'Farrell, a woman Charlotte no longer fears, no longer envies. A woman she feels pity for. As she sets a journal atop the stack beside her, the pile of books shudders then crashes to the floor. With a sigh Charlotte gathers them together, then notices a slip of paper peeking out from the pages of one of the journals. The journal was dated fifteen years ago, the first of its number. And inside it is a letter.

*Dear Ellis.*

Charlotte stops reading at once. She feels as if she is spying, overhearing a conversation not meant for her ears. Though she knows it is wrong, she can't help but read.

*Dear Ellis,*

*By the time you are reading this I am gone. I know you would not be so sentimental as to read through these journals while I was still with you. You never wanted to know exactly what I was thinking, you preferred to see me as someone better than I was, more beautiful, more perfect. I am not perfect. No, no, don't sully my memory by idealizing me, only remembering the best parts of me. I want you to remember it all, the good and the bad. I want you to remember me as I was, flawed but trying my best. I don't want you to think of me as some angel, peaceful, finally at rest after a long battle. If anything I am a restless spirit. I am angry. Angry that the future I had planned for myself is no longer a possibility. You know how important my work is to me. You know how I have always wanted to make a name for myself, to*

        **MEAGAN CLEVELAND**

*prove that I mattered. But you and I both know that I didn't, not to them. You and I both know that if I were to submit my work with my name attached it would lay forgotten in a drawer, gathering dust. We both know that our professors never expected me to succeed, to them I was just your shadow, your echo. Do you remember what Dr. Kowalski said to me? That I was there for an MRS not an MA?*

*They never believed I had anything worthwhile to stay. They thought I was there to find a man, to get married, that Art History was a hobby I would soon outgrow. But you, you were always the one they rooted for, the one they believed was going places. You were their ideal student, the worthy successor. I know my work is important, not just to me, but to the discipline itself. But if I were the one to present it, no one would take it seriously. I want you to publish it. If I had lived long enough to finish my PhD I would be Dr. O'Farrell too. Publish my work Ellis. Publish it in your name. It will be my last laugh.*

*Please do this one last thing for me.*

*If you need further convincing, go to my mother. She always had a way of convincing you to do what was right.*

*Love always,*

*Antoinette*

Charlotte reads the letter once, then a second, then a third time. Hardly believing the words. Antoinette O'Farrell *wanted* him to publish her work in his name?

Judging from the contents of the letter, it sounded as if Antoinette's experience of Thornfield was less than ideal. Charlotte was fortunate that she had not experienced sexism while in the department, but the letter proved it was not always this way. She mourns the person Antoinette O'Farrell could have become, if her illness and bitterness had not overtaken her. A brilliant scholar making a better environment for her students, someone like Cat. But Antoinette is just a memory.

Charlotte folds the letter and slips it into her pocket. She gathers together the journals and places them back into the box. She carries it upstairs and outside to the waiting taxi idling on the driveway. She opens the door, places the box within and asks the driver to take her to one more stop before her final destination.

The driver pulls up at another house very similar to Dr. O' Farrell's. A square, Georgian Style house with rows of symmetrical windows and chimneys. But this home is not open and inviting like Dr. O' Farrell's, no, here the curtains are closed against the light, the roof shingles painted in a dour grey. Charlotte recognizes the beautiful garden she had seen on Dr. O' Farrell's Twitter account, flower beds spilling with roses, dahlias, peonies and hydrangeas in splendid shades of pink. Charlotte lifts her burden and carries it up the gravel path and to the front door. She rings the bell and waits.

Her arms tremble with the weight of the box, but she does not set it on the ground.

 **MEAGAN CLEVELAND**

Eventually she hears movement on the other side of the door, she sees the curtains peel back and a white face peer out before the curtains snap shut once more. She hears the lock turn in the door and it opens.

Mrs. Mason looks like a completely different woman than the one Charlotte had met all those months ago. Her face, which was once so carefully made up is free of make-up, the early morning light highlighting every crease and wrinkle. Her head is covered by a silk scarf, and despite the rising heat of the morning, she is wearing a woollen sweater. Though there is a marked difference in her appearance her attitude seems to have not changed. She sizes Charlotte up with the same level of scrutiny.

"Can I help you?"

"I thought you might like these?" Charlotte glances down at the box in her trembling arms. Mrs. Mason looks at the box, sighs and retreats into the house. Charlotte takes this as an invitation and follows her inside.

The house is in slight disarray. A thin coating of dust clings to each surface, dust motes dance in the thin stream of summer light that slices through the gap in the closed curtains.

"Well? What do you want?" Mrs. Mason demands rather rudely.

Charlotte gently sets the box down on the floor and removes the lid.

Mrs. Mason's voice hitches once she catches sight of the journals. She leans down, her fingers trailing over the initials on the corners.

"Where did you get these?"

"From Dr. O' Farrell's house."

"I thought they were destroyed in the fire." She murmurs, lifting one of the journals and leafing through its pages. Her face softens as she reads the familiar handwriting. She remembers Charlotte's presence and her face hardens once more. "Dr. O' Farrell, hm? I thought the two of you would be on a first name basis after that cozy scene I interrupted."

"There seems to be a misunderstanding. There is nothing going on between us."

Mrs. Mason raises a brow. "Oh? I did not know it was common for my son-in-law to hold sleepovers with his students."

"I'm not his student. I was his teaching assistant."

"Same difference. You should not have been there with him. He's a married man."

"He's not. Not any more."

Mrs. Mason flinches at Charlotte's words. The journal drops from her hand. With difficulty, she bends to retrieve it, the same moment Charlotte does, their fingertips touching as they both reach for the journal. Mrs. Mason looks up at Charlotte, her eyes brimming with tears.

"What do you want?" She repeats.

"I wanted to bring this last piece of your daughter back to you."

Mrs. Mason snatches the journal from Charlotte's grasp and holds it close.

"Well, you've brought them back." She snaps. And then she grudgingly adds, "I had given these to Ellis. I thought he would want to look through them. To publish more of Antoinette's work."

 

"You knew about that?" Charlotte asks, surprised. And then she remembers the last line of the letter.

*If you need further convincing, go to my mother. She always had a way of convincing you to do what was right.*

"Of course I knew about that. I have been trying to get Ellis to publish more of Toni's work for years. But this box has sat in his basement just as long, collecting dust. I may have been putting too much pressure on him to keep my daughter's memory alive.  Over the past few years he has become a vehicle, a living embodiment of Toni's memory. I know that it isn't fair to him to keep doing this to him. He has his own thoughts, his own ideas, his own passions. I know that he can't keep living for a ghost anymore." She glares at Charlotte. "I suppose that's where you come in?"

Charlotte stands tall against her scrutiny. She does not flinch at her words. "Can you tell me where to find him?"

Mrs. Mason glares at her a little longer. Then she gently sets the journal down atop the others and walks slowly over to a table by the front entrance to a pad of paper and a pen. She jots down an address and hands it wordlessly to Charlotte.

"Thank you."

Mrs. Mason turns her back on Charlotte, clearly done with the interaction. But Charlotte does not leave, not yet.

"For what it's worth, I think Antoinette would have been a great scholar." Charlotte says.

Mrs. Mason does not turn, however, her shoulders lose a little of their tension.

"Of course she would have. She was the best."

"Goodbye, Mrs Mason."

Charlotte shuts the door on her way out. The sky has darkened and a storm is brewing on the horizon.

She clutches the piece of paper in her hands like a lifeline.

She has to see him again.

　　　　MEAGAN CLEVELAND

# CHAPTER THIRTY ONE

## RECONCILIATIONIS

It is raining once the taxi pulls up at the hospital and Charlotte's tears mingle with the raindrops. A fierce wind whips her hair in every direction around her. Strands catch on her tearstained cheeks and Charlotte continually reaches up to push the wet strands away from her face. The morning air is clammy against her skin but she barely feels it. Her body is numb as she stands before the hospital doors. Her best friend, her mentor, *her love*, is within those walls. She does not know how to face him after the months that have separated them. The sound of the rain pounding against the glass resounds in her head. Even though the world is wet, her mouth feels dry. A lump forms in her throat as if her heart is trying to rise from her and join Dr. O' Farrell in his hospital bed. Charlotte clamps her mouth shut. Her heart is her own.

Charlotte smells rich earth, recently mown grass, the damp summer air, all mingled with the perfume of hand sanitizer. Charlotte takes a breath and steps through the sliding glass doors.

Dr. O' Farrell is in the recovery unit. Charlotte drifts over to the map by the elevator and locates where she needs to go. With a ding, the elevator doors open and Charlotte slips inside.

She grips a bouquet of flowers in her hands, trying not to grasp the stems too tightly or crush the petals. The doors swish open and Charlotte makes her way down the brightly lit hallway. She tries not to look into the open doorways, to give its occupants some peace from her prying eyes. She quickly glances at room numbers and then away, silently counting in her head until she reaches the room number written on the slip of paper in her pocket. She pauses outside the open door, not daring to peer inside. She takes another breath, deep through her nose, and out through her mouth. She raps her knuckles on the door.

"Bugger off." A sullen voice calls from within.

She cannot help the smile that blooms on her face.

Cautiously, she makes her way inside. The curtain has been drawn around the bed, shielding its occupant from view. She pauses hesitantly at the curtain's edge.

"Well? Have you come to torture me yet again?" That familiar voice says.

Charlotte takes this as an invitation and pushes back the curtain.

She stifles a gasp.

Dr. O' Farrell is stretched out on the bed on his back. His arm in a sling, his leg propped up in a cast. Half his face is covered in gauze, his left eye is covered, the other stares straight ahead at the ceiling.

"Well? Get on with it nurse."

Charlotte clears her throat. "You once said I wasn't a nurse."

At the sound of her voice Dr. O' Farrell jerks his head to the side. His gaze holds her own and she sees his eyes well up with tears.

  

"What the hell have they given me this time?" He mutters. "Now I am seeing things."

"Hearing things too," Charlotte adds cheerfully. She steps closer to the bed and leans down to set the flowers on the bedside table.

"Are you real?" He whispers.

She is glad he cannot see her face, as her own eyes well with tears. She hastily wipes them away and straightens.

"Oh I'm real, alright. And I am here for answers."

Dr. O' Farrell gestures with his good hand. "Is now really the moment?"

Charlotte glowers in response.

"What do you want to ask?"

"It's not what I want to ask. It's what you want to say to me. Now's your chance to explain yourself." Charlotte crosses her arms and waits expectantly.

Dr. O' Farrell sighs and gestures at the chair in the corner, within sight of his good eye. Charlotte walks across the room and sinks into the uncomfortable chair.

"It's good to see you." He says. Charlotte can feel a smile pulling at the corner of her mouth but suppresses it. She isn't going to make it easy for him. His own smile broadens at her reaction. "Still giving me the silent treatment Grey?"

"This is your last chance to explain. Better quit stalling."

He chuckles in response, his hand going to the controls of his bed to raise the mattress so he can look at her better.

"Where to start?"

"How about the journals."

"In the basement? My mother-in-law gave them to me after Antoinette died. She, Antoinette, not Bertha, wanted me to *keep her memory alive.*" He makes air quotes with his good hand at the words.

"By passing off her research as your own?" Charlotte replies, trying not to wince at the tone of her voice.

"Yes, that. She asked me to. Antoinette wanted to be a professor her entire life. She was so excited to start grad school. She was excited about everything, she had such a passion for her studies, for her interests. She lit up whenever she got to talk about art. But, once she started grad school, she lost that light.

"They were *horrible* to her. Horrible. They offered every opportunity to me, inviting me to parties, introducing me to colleagues, accepting my papers for conferences and giving me all the best grades. Just because of my sex, who I was related to back home. But her? They excluded her at every turn. Rejected her papers, tried to fail her, but even they couldn't find fault with her test results. They had to find other ways to snub her. Cat and I, in recent years, we've actively tried to make Thornfield a better, more inclusive place. But it wasn't always that way. Thornfield prided itself on being a serious place, for serious people, to embark on serious pursuits. And as a young woman, they would never consider Antoinette as a serious scholar."

"But what about Cat? She was in your cohort too, wasn't she?"

"You wouldn't think it to look at her now, but they treated Cat the same as they treated Antoinette. As lesser than, not worthy to be there. Unserious. A diversity stunt and not much more. But Cat is *strong.* She fought them at every turn. She showed up to class in her pink dresses and her curled hair

    MEAGAN CLEVELAND

and she dominated every discussion, aced every exam. She was so strong. But Antoinette wasn't. They broke her. It got worse when she was sick. She was so angry all the time. She had to take a leave of absence but insisted that I continue, that I get my degree in spite of everything. Near the end I thought she hated me for it, getting what she always wanted for herself. So when I saw the letter I was so relieved. She wasn't angry at me, but at *them*. If I did what she wanted, she would be happy. So I did it. I hated it, but I did it to keep her words alive. And all these years, these men who had read her exams, her papers, they never once put it together that it was her. She was right in the end, they didn't see her, didn't appreciate how smart she was. They would only acknowledge her work if a man's name, if *my* name was attached. And all these years, they've been waiting for my next great article, the successor to my great work. But it wasn't mine you see? It wasn't my words, my ideas they loved but hers. Do you know how it felt to write anything after that? For all my own work to be judged as inferior to that initial article? To know that I was a fraud? There was a time I thought that I was the one who should have died, that she should have lived on in my place. The world needed her more than me.

"And then I met you. On the side of the road, emerging out of a nightmare was this beautiful person, worried about *me*. It had been so long since anyone truly saw me. You see me Charlotte, better than anyone. I'm sorry if you hate me for what I've done."

Exhausted from his speech he rests his head back and closes his eye. A tear trails down his cheek, he goes to wipe it away but, one arm is in a sling, the other is attached to an

IV with limited motion. He huffs in frustration and turns his face away.

Moved to tears herself, Charlotte stands and approaches the bed. Gently, she wipes the tear away with a trembling finger. He turns towards her, his expression hopeful.

"I see you."

He nods. He knows that. "But do you forgive me?"

Charlotte reaches into her pocket and withdraws the letter.

Dr. O' Farrell sees it. He looks from the letter to her. Mock outrage on his face.

"You made me make that speech when you knew the truth all along?"

Charlotte shrugs, placing the letter back into her pocket. "You said you wanted to explain."

Dr. O' Farrell begins to laugh then just as quickly stops with a groan, his good arm reaching for his injured shoulder.

"Ow. Don't make me laugh, Grey. It hurts."

"I can tell you off some more if you prefer."

He chuckles in response, holding his shoulder as he laughs.

Charlotte sits at the foot of his bed.

"So. If you could start all over again, what would you write about?"

His laughter is cut short. He regards her warily before he speaks.

"Not the Renaissance. I hate that stuff."

Charlotte raises her brows in surprise.

"Really? You know so much about it."

"Yes, and it bores the hell out of me."

"What would you write about instead?"

     **MEAGAN CLEVELAND**

He hesitates.

She reaches for his hand and holds it in hers.

He smiles.

"Modern art. Dadaism, abstract expressionism, cubism, you know, the weird stuff."

"The weird stuff." She repeats with a laugh. "So do that. Write about modern art, teach it even. You don't have to be in Antoinette's shadow anymore."

The tears flow freely now. His breath hitches as he suppresses a sob and Charlotte leans forward to press her lips against his.

"And once you start teaching modern art, there will be a vacancy for the Renaissance class that I can take over."

He laughs through tears, reaching for her with his good hand to bring her face to his once more.

"Move on from one woman to another?" He murmurs. "Shall I stand in your shadow now, Grey?"

Charlotte shakes her head. "No, not in my shadow. I don't want you to stand behind me. I want you to stand me, Ellis."

He presses his forehead into the curve between her shoulder and neck, and she wraps her arms around him, holding him close.

The bond between them mended once more.

# ACKNOWLEDGEMENTS

Writers are often solitary creatures, however this writer is enormously thankful to the many people who have supported me and my writing over the years.

To Holly, thank you for creating the stunning cover for Thornfield. It has been a joy to work with you again.

To my AO3 readers, thank you for your kudos and your love for my writing. Thank you to Catherine (captainofthegreenpeas) especially for your edits and notes.

To Jen, thank you for our long phone calls, one of which gave me the idea for Thornfield in the first place!

To Amanda for the stories told in the dark when we were supposed to be sleeping, for the endless Barbie dramas, and for the book swapping, thank you for sharing your love of storytelling with me. Amanda is the most creative person I know and has inspired my love of writing. One day we'll see the Four Enchantments on the page!

To Andrew for our chats about movies and musicals and finding inspiration on the stage and the screen. Andrew is the bravest person I know, thank you for showing me how to put myself out there.

To Allison for always championing me and my work, thank you for the years of anime and k-drama watching and for sharing all your favourite manga with me. Writing romance isn't so hard when you've read as much Shōjo manga as us! Allison works harder than anyone I know and I admire her work ethic.

To Melanie, my partner in crime, for the nights sharing our life's dreams and making them a reality. Melanie is the most resilient person I know, she inspires me to keep dreaming and to keep trying no matter what it takes.

To my Dad who encourages me to take risks, work hard and celebrates my wins. My dad is my role model and I strive to be more like him.

To my Mum, who is the most loving person I know. Her love gives me the incentive to keep writing and make the world as magical as she made my childhood.

To my Nan for being my biggest fan, for the nightly phone calls, for always knowing I could do it and not being surprised at all when I achieve my goals.

To my Grandad who is the most supportive person in my life, for always believing in me and supporting me no matter what.

To Richard for  encouraging me to do my best and be my best, I don't know where I would be without you.

And to Henry, thank you for making my world and my dreams bigger and richer than I could have imagined.

# ABOUT THE AUTHOR

Meagan is an author and classicist. Meagan's MA and BA in Classics have taken her on many adventures: attending a week-long conference speaking exclusively in Latin, living with archaeologists in Rome, delivering a paper on Greek tragedy at a conference at Oxford, and searching for the Sphinx in modern Thebes. Aside from writing, Meagan loves reading, watching period dramas and bullet journalling. Meagan lives in London Ontario with her husband, son, and cat.